Letters in the Attic

Letters in the Attic

BONNIE SHIMKO

ACADEMY
CHICAGO

Published in 2007 by
Academy Chicago Publishers
363 West Erie Street
Chicago, Illinois 60610

Hardcover edition printed in 2002.

© 2002 by Bonnie Shimko

Printed in Canada

Library of Congress Cataloging-in-Publication Data

Shimko, Bonnie.
  Letters in the attic / Bonnie Shimko.
    p. cm.
  ISBN 0-89733-511-2 (cloth)
  ISBN 978-0-89733-563-8 (paper)
   1. Girls—Fiction. 2. Single parent families—Fiction. 3. Mothers
and daughters--Fiction. 4. Grandparent and child—Fiction. 5. New York
(State)—Fiction. I. Title.
  PS3619.H57 L48 2002
  813'.6—dc21
                                            2002007854

For my daughter, Sarah, with love

———◆———

"To me, each cloud in summertime
Is silver—never gray
For to truly love a rainbow
We must learn to love the rain."
—T.J. Lanaghan

CHAPTER ONE

———

MAMA'S GONE BACK to Phoenix again tonight. She's talking in her sleep, so I know exactly what the nightmare is about. It's the same one she always has after she reads the letters. If they were mine, I would stop reading them and get a good night's rest. Better yet, I would throw them in the burn barrel and let that be the end of it.

She doesn't think I know what she's dreaming about, and she puts on a good show while I'm standing by the couch in my grandmother's living room, shaking her awake. "Oh, Lizzy, it was horrible!" she says, grabbing at the air for my hand. "I was in the woods and wild animals were chasing me. I shouldn't have eaten that sardine sandwich before I went to bed."

What she doesn't realize is that I have a very good memory—one that takes me back to when I was a baby in a crib—or nearly. I was much older than a baby in a crib when the dream she is lying to me about was made, so I have a perfect recollection of everything that happened.

She is not in the woods and no wild animals are chasing her. She's in our hotel room, and my father is standing over her bed, telling her he wants a divorce. The worst part of the whole thing is that the reason for his wanting a divorce is right next to him, holding his hand.

There is poor Mama—looking like Hazel from the television show, only worse because she is done up for night—not knowing that she would be entertaining Daddy's new girlfriend, who I hate to admit, looks like a million dollars in a dime store sort of way.

It's Mama's night off and she's in bed reading with the lamp tilted toward her. Her hair is in curlers and her face is covered in Pond's cold cream. The bulb in that lamp is a spotlight, making the cold cream shine like Crisco. She's wearing her everyday nightie—the one with the grape juice stain on the front from when I tripped while I was bringing her breakfast in bed on her birthday. Even soaking it in cold water and the foolproof recipe from Dear Heloise would not get that stain out.

The woman who is stealing her husband is all dressed up with makeup on, looking down at her and smiling. To make matters even worse—the harlot, which is the name Mama uses when she is referring to her, is about fifteen years younger and the size of the runway model Mama keeps a picture of on the refrigerator to remind herself not to open the door.

The grown-ups in that room are counting on me to be asleep on the cot in the corner behind the folding screen, which lets us have a two-bedroom suite without paying a king's ransom. What they don't know is that I can see everything that's going on because the cloth on that screen is old and there are a lot of worn-out places that make perfect peepholes. I have always been a good actress about pretending to be asleep. I know not to let my eyelids flutter and to breathe in a slow and even rhythm. Why, you wouldn't believe the information I have stored away in my head because of being such a good actress.

When my father, who works as a bartender downstairs, and the harlot first come into the room, he leans over me to see if I'm sleeping. He pulls the covers up around my chin, which is exactly what I don't want because the room is an oven since we're on the cheap side of the hotel with no air conditioning. Pulling the covers up is just a show he's putting on for *her,* because if he were alone and not trying to make a good impression, my bed could be on fire and he wouldn't bother himself to get a glass of water to save me. I hear him tell her my name and that I'm eleven years old, which is wrong because I've been twelve for more than six months.

My real name is Elizabeth after Elizabeth Taylor, which Mama shortened to Lizzy because she thinks it's cute. Personally, I think it's an ugly name and I will never shorten my kids' beautiful names to something ugly—that is if I have any, which I most likely will not. To start out with a beautiful name like Elizabeth and end up with Lizzy is a hard pill to swallow. You can imagine how often I'm called Lizard by the dumb boys in school who are trying to impress their friends by making fun of somebody.

I would never complain about my name to Mama because she cries easily. You would think that a person who has been insulted and belittled all her life by her own mother and then by her own husband would have grown a thicker skin. She will even cry if I make a mistake and mention that the toast is dry. It doesn't matter that I have toasted it myself—she thinks it's her fault for buying the wrong bread.

My father and the harlot stand at the bottom of her bed, so I can see all the characters in the play—just like I have paid extra for a front row seat. The first thing my father does is to tell Mama to cover herself—can't she see she has a visitor?

"Vonnie," he says, "I would like you to meet a friend of mine. This is Sylvia Bushey. She's a hatcheck girl over at the Flamingo."

Sylvia Bushey and hatcheck girl—if you don't count the way they look, Mama is ahead by two. A name like Sylvia Bushey can't compare to Veronica McMann and a hatcheck girl is a far cry from a professional piano player, even if it is only at the Sunrise Hotel. But—the Sunrise Hotel is a big step down from the Flamingo, so if you look at it *that* way, she's really only ahead by one.

"I want a divorce," he goes on. "Sylvia and I are in love and we're going to get married." He waits for a reaction and when none comes, he continues. "Now, don't go falling apart. You know as well as me that things haven't been good between us for a long time."

As far as I can see, she is not falling apart or doing anything at all for that matter. She is sitting up in bed clutching her book to her chest, not moving a muscle. It's hard to see the expression on her face because of the cold cream, but her ice blue eyes are darting back and forth as if she's watching a tennis game—first at my father and then at the harlot.

"Say something," he whines. "Don't be like that."

Her eyes are still now and she looks like a stage-frightened mime being gawked at by an unwelcome audience.

"We don't have all day," my father informs her. "Buster's holding down the bar for me and Sylvia here is on break and has to get back. She was nice enough to take the time to come over and meet you. The least you can do is be cordial."

My father and the harlot exchange looks and then he goes on. "Well, Vonnie, if you're going to be like that, there's nothing more I can do. I'm going to clear my things out now and I'll get the papers to you in the morning. Just put your John Hancock on the dotted line and get them back to me. Sylvia and I will run down to Mexico and it'll be over with just like that." While he's saying the word *that,* he snaps his fingers like a magician to show just how easily he can make Mama's marriage disappear into thin air.

I couldn't swear to it in a court of law because my eyes are closed, but I don't think he even looks in my direction on his way out the door, which proves what I have always known—Manny McMann is not cut out to be anybody's father. If that's what Sylvia Bushey is looking for, she's going to be very disappointed.

I wait a minute, and then I pretend that the door closing brought me out of a deep sleep. I make little waking-up noises, and then I head toward the bathroom. On my way, I glance over and see that Mama has not moved an inch and is staring straight ahead at the fake painting of some famous artist's jug

of flowers, which is screwed to the wall in case we get it into
our heads to steal it. While I'm in the bathroom, I flush to make
it seem as if I needed to go. Then I run water in the sink, but I
don't see any reason to wash my hands since they haven't been
anywhere to get dirty.

I take the book out of Mama's hand and turn out the light. I
go around the bed, crawl in on Manny's side, and put my head
on the pillow so it is touching her arm. I take hold of her hand
and wait for the crying to start, because what has just happened
is a lot worse than dry toast. I fight the sleep that is coming so
I can keep her company and get Kleenex for her tears. When I
wake up the next morning, she is still staring at those flowers
and her eyes are dry.

CHAPTER TWO

———◆———

I'M IN THE KITCHENETTE making coffee—the same as every morning. The kitchenette is the reason the front desk can call our room a suite and can charge sixty dollars a month for rent. I take the milk out of the refrigerator and give it a whiff. A little off is okay, but today there are chunks, and that means Mama will have to take her coffee black. After what she has been through, chunky milk is sure to put her over the edge.

It would be nice to be able to buy the school cafeteria-size at the market because a whole quart is sure to turn sour before a person can use that much milk to lighten her coffee. Manny takes his the blacker the better, and my system cannot tolerate milk in any form, so we're no help in using it up before it goes bad.

Mama's afraid I'll grow up with a skeleton that resembles a pretzel because she has read somewhere that kids who don't drink their milk end up with rickets. I'm taking my chances on that one. I would rather end up a little crooked than having to run to the bathroom every ten minutes.

I wish the hotel would fix our refrigerator. If we don't remember to pound on it every few hours, whatever is in it gets ruined. Manny thinks it's the fan that's sticking, but he says it's not his

job to fix it and it'll be a cold day in you know where before
he'll pay a repairman.

I'm not sure how I will handle the scene that is just around
the corner, so I keep myself busy by rearranging the silverware
drawer and try not to think about it. Just as the percolator
begins to burp, Mama comes in. I tell her about the sour milk
and I wait for her to fall apart.

"Lizzy," she says, "it's a beautiful day. It would be a shame to
waste it by staying inside. Why don't we go out for breakfast?"

She's in such a good mood that I think maybe I dreamed what
went on last night, or maybe my father came back while I was
sleeping and told her he was just kidding about the divorce and
that he will love her forever. I take a chance and say, "I crawled
in with you last night. I was a little lonely by myself. Where's
Manny? Is he asleep in my bed?"

"No," she says, not looking at me. "Didn't I tell you? Manny
had to work a double shift and he didn't want to disturb us, so
he stayed in Buster's room. I'm sure he'll be here when we get
back from breakfast. We'll have to remember to bring something for him."

I'm used to hearing lies about Manny's spending the night
in Buster's room to save us from being disturbed, so I don't act
surprised and I don't ask any questions.

Mama's a stickler for good hygiene and I have followed her
lead, so it takes us a while to get ready to go out—even if it's
just to the coffee shop downstairs. She bought me my own jar of
Tussy deodorant, so if my body shifts gears on me in the middle
of any given day, I will be prepared. She tells me that any time
now I will turn from a little girl into a woman, and when that
happens, I will hold an odor if I'm not careful. It's better to be
safe than sorry—that's her motto.

"Remember, Lizzy," she has told me a thousand times, "there
is no reason for anybody to go around with an offensive odor
in this day and age—soap and water are cheap." For us, they're
better than cheap. The front desk can't tell us how much hot

water to use because our faucets are attached to the rest of the water in the hotel. As far as soap—Mama is not above going for a little stroll in the better part of the hotel and taking a handful off the maid's wagon when she's not looking. Because our suite is in the not-done-over section of the hotel, which is occupied mostly by the help and people who are down on their luck, we don't get maid service or guest soaps. Mama thinks that is discrimination. There's nothing she can do about the maid service, but she *can* do something about the soap. If you squeeze five or six of those little Ivorys together and then smooth out the edges, you can get yourself a decent-size bar.

You would think that a family of three, with both parents working, would be able to afford a decent place to live—maybe even a small rented house in a moderate neighborhood with a backyard big enough for a barbecue grill and a picnic table. One of those put-together-yourself pools so the kid in the family could keep herself cool in the stifling Arizona heat should not be too much to ask. That *would* be the case if the father of the family didn't see a sure thing around every corner and didn't lose his shirt every time he turned around. It would also help if the cheapskate hotel the mother works for would pay her a salary instead of making her work for just tips.

"It's so humiliating," Mama tells me more often than I want to hear it. "Having that jar sitting on the piano makes me feel like a beggar."

Sometimes, the only money that gets put into that jar the whole night is the dollar bill she puts in it herself to prime the pump.

"You mark my words," she says, tapping the table with her index finger. "Someday I'll have a respectable job. Maybe even a music teacher in a school with health insurance and a pension plan. You just mark my words."

I don't have the heart to tell her that she would have to have a certificate of some kind to work in a school—not just the fact that she was Miss Lucy Simpson's prize pupil from the second grade until she graduated high school.

While I'm waiting for Mama to finish in the bathroom, I do up our beds. Then I go about tidying up the rest of the room. I don't know the name of the book she's reading until I turn it right side up on the nightstand. Below the words *Passion Before Midnight*, there's a picture of a man and a woman on the cover. The man is holding the woman tightly around her waist and is looking down at her with a Clark Gable face—the one he wears in *Gone with the Wind* where he thinks he's such a big deal around Scarlett O'Hara, always locking her in a vise hug and smash kissing her to prove his point.

Personally, Clark Gable is not my type, even if he were my age or a little older. I am not crazy about tall, dark and hand-some—and especially not mustaches. If I were in the market for a boyfriend, I would go more for the Russ Tamblyn type—cute and blond and not scary-looking at all—just regular nice-look-ing, plus a good dancer.

The woman is wearing a long red gown with no sleeves and not enough top to speak of. Her head is thrown back, and her long black curls are flowing over her enormous breasts, which are all but falling out of that dress. You expect one of them to fly out any second and give Clark Gable a black eye. She has a look on her face that says she is carrying the weight of the world on her shoulders and does not know where to turn.

When I hold the book at arm's length and squinch my eyes, I could swear it's my father on the cover of that book with his arms around the harlot—except the harlot was not wearing a long gown when she stood at the bottom of Mama's bed, and my father is a far cry from Clark Gable except for the same mustache. It's amazing what poor eyesight and a good imagina-tion can do. Mama has gotten as far as chapter twelve. There are cold cream stains on the page where she stopped reading when Manny dropped the bomb on her.

I just get started reading words that are not for twelve-year-old eyes when she comes out of the bathroom. She's wearing the dress she got married in—the yellow print with the low

ruffled front and see-through sleeves—the one that is so small,
I'm embarrassed for her.

Right here, I have a dilemma on my hands. The only mirror
we have is the one over the sink in the bathroom, so Mama can
only see the top part of herself. She has to trust her luck for the
rest. I'm trying to decide whether to tell her that her back end
has a mind of its own in that dress. It's like a scared animal
trying to fight its way out of a paper bag. The hem is hiked up
so far in the back that her slip is hanging down a foot. This is
way more than snowing down south—this is a blizzard! I decide
to leave well enough alone. She is doing very well considering,
and besides, her slip is nothing to be ashamed of. It is white like
the after-picture in a Clorox ad, as if to say, this is the color an
undergarment is supposed to be—look at it and learn.

"Lizzy," she says, "you know I don't like you reading
grown-up books. Here, I'll just tuck that under my pillow for
tonight."

What she doesn't realize is that I could *write* a grown-up
book from the information I have stored away in my head from
peeking through the worn spots on that folding screen by my
bed when she and my father have counted on me to be asleep.
It is very hard to stay asleep while bedsprings are squealing
and Mama is calling out, "Manny . . . Oh, Manny . . . You are
the king!"

CHAPTER THREE

———◆———

THE COFFEE SHOP IS sit-any-place-you-please, so we take a booth by the window. This turns out to be a mistake, because there are a million dead flies on the windowsill, lying on their backs with their legs in the air as if they are saying, *Watch out! This is what happens if you eat here.* If you ask me, this is poor advertising on the part of the management. People walking by, trying to decide whether to come in would shade their eyes, peer in, and *YOW! Dead flies all over the place . . . not going to eat here.* How hard could it be to wet a wad of toilet paper and give those flies a decent burial is what I would like to know. My hands are washed and ready, so I'm going to forget about it.

There's a television set bolted to the wall above the counter like the one in our suite, only this one is color and there are no squiggly lines to make you sick when you watch it. President Kennedy is on, playing with his little daughter Caroline in their backyard. Now *that's* what I call a backyard. You never get to see it, but I bet their swimming pool is the kind you see movie stars sitting around in *Photoplay*—the kidney-shaped ones with a fountain in the middle and a platform for diving off.

Mrs. Kennedy always makes sure Caroline is just right—short white dress, matching socks and shoes—the real leather two-

strap kind that fancy little kids in England wear—and a floppy
white bow to finish everything off. You could never find anything even a little bit smudgy about her. I bet at night—Bam!
Everything she had on that day gets thrown away, and tomorrow
there will be a whole new outfit.

"He reminds me of Manny." Mama has a look on her face
that makes me think, *Oh, boy . . . I bet she's going to blow. I
have to take this slow and easy.*

"Who reminds you of Manny?" I ask, searching the coffee
shop.

"President Kennedy. He looks just like Manny."

Well, now, this is going to take some acting. "You know,
Mama, you're right. I never noticed it before."

While she watches Manny play with Caroline Kennedy on the
White House lawn, I picture Mrs. Kennedy and Manny out on a
date. There she would be—all perfect in a real wool suit, probably
blue or maybe white, with a pillbox hat and expensive shoes—the
kind that you can't tell where the sole leaves off and the heel
starts—with a purse to match. And there would be Manny—just
the opposite. He would be wearing his wedding suit that has been
hanging in the back of the closet next to Mama's yellow dress
since the day we moved to Phoenix. He has added a couple of
spare tires, so the jacket of that suit would not be buttoned. If
it was a Friday night date, his hair would have taken on a patent leather look and his deodorant would have given up trying,
because he still follows the hygiene rules he grew up with. You
take a bath on Saturday night plus a shampoo, and after that—I
guess a skunk really can't smell his own stink.

I'm picturing the look on Mrs. Kennedy's face after Manny
pinches her bottom and says, *How about it, babe?* when I hear
Mama say, "Oh good. She's coming. I need some coffee."

When the waitress arrives at our table, she has the same sour
look on her face she always wears when she waits on us. Her
Pepto-Bismol pink uniform has a safety pin on the front where
one of the buttons has popped off. She didn't even bother to pin

it from the inside so just a sliver of silver would show through and maybe nobody would notice. There it is—the size you would use to pin a diaper on a baby and she doesn't even care. On top of that, it isn't even new. It's so rusted that you'd have to go to the doctor for a tetanus shot if it stabbed you. You can tell by how she's put together that under the top of her uniform is a bra your mother wouldn't want you to be wearing if you got in a car wreck. The hairnet she has on makes the curls on her head look like smashed sausages—the small kind that come with pancakes. On top of the sausages, she has bobby-pinned a pink head thing the size of a Band-Aid, which makes me think—what is the point of that? The bobby pins are black and the jagged kind. Against the pink Band-Aid, they remind me of something that would crawl in the dirt—like when you turn a rock over and there they are—all long and creepy.

This is a time when it would be nice to be with another girl my own age so that we could make fun of the situation. With Mama, I have to keep a straight face and act as if I don't notice anything that's just begging for a smart remark.

Now, it would be a completely different story if she came to the table with a smile and said *Good morning, ladies. How are you today? What can I get for you?* That way you would look past the flaws and you would be extra nice so that she wouldn't feel embarrassed about her shortcomings in the attire department. You wouldn't *want* to make fun of her. You would make up all kinds of excuses for her like, *poor thing . . . she probably can't afford a new safety pin*, and things like that.

Mama orders a side of toast and coffee with extra cream. I add that she likes grape jelly, which is a lie because she doesn't take anything on her toast except a slather of butter. I know if I leave it up to Miss Pepto-Bismol, we will get marmalade for sure, because Mama looks like the marmalade type. It's beyond me why anybody would want to spread orange rinds on their toast when they're what you throw in the garbage before you start on the good part. Even worse than marmalade is apple jelly. I don't know who came up with that idea, but it certainly was a bust. As far as I'm concerned, you might just as well pee on your toast. You would have the same flavor and you could save some money. I remind the waitress about the grape jelly so that it will stick in her memory. She gives me a dirty look, then stands on one foot so she can scratch that ankle with her other shoe.

When it's my turn, we go through the same routine as always. Mama studies the menu as if she's cramming for a test. She coaxes me to order something—an omelet or maybe some French toast with bacon. I refuse, saying that I couldn't manage a bite. I'm just here to keep Mama company. She gives the waitress a look that says, *Well, I tried, what more can I do?* The waitress rolls her eyes to let us know she isn't fooled. Then she turns on her heel and heads toward the counter to place our order.

When the food comes, there's a soup bowl full of marmalade packets. The waitress drops it on the table and glares at me like she's asking if I want to make something of it, and if I do, she'll meet me in the alley after her shift is over. I don't push my luck because I can tell she's like the girls at school who smoke in the bathroom, only grown up.

We each have a slice of toast and I get first go at the coffee because of the milk thing—even a little bit can throw me off. One cup is all I can manage, and when I'm done, Mama asks for a free fill up and more cream please. She has packed the creamers from the first cup safely away in her purse for tomorrow.

When we're finished, she puts a dime under her plate. We don't waste any time leaving because a dime is a slap in the face tip and we don't want to be sitting there when the waitress finds it. I don't know why we kill ourselves trying to escape, because every waitress in the place has our number. *Here they are—the big spenders!* They probably draw straws when they see us coming in the door.

So far so good—things with Mama are still going in a straight line. We go across the street to the bakery to buy a jelly doughnut for Manny. They're his favorite, and he has told me more than once to run out and get him one. It would never occur to him to ask me if I would like a little something sweet or if I could pick up something for Mama while I'm there. He does a very good job of taking care of himself and he makes sure the people around him do the same. "I hope this is fresh," he says every time I bring a doughnut back for him, not even offering to share a bite. When I tell him it is, he squeezes the bag to see if I'm lying. After the squeeze, he lets out a grunt that says Okay . . . *now* I believe you, but you'd better watch it the *next* time. If there's change, he counts it to the last penny to make sure I haven't broken the law and treated myself to a candy bar or maybe a pack of gum.

I hold the bakery door open for Mama. She takes one step and runs smack into a balloon. Music is coming from a hidden radio—*Begin the Beguine*. It's as if somebody is throwing us a surprise party, like they've been waiting for us to come. Balloons and crepe paper garlands are all over the place. It's raining happiness in here.

Before we even get to the counter, a clown comes up to us and holds out a tray of French pastries—the ones that look like private little birthday cakes. Mama asks, "How much?" The clown tells her the cakes are free. The bakery is five years old today.

Well, what do you know! We're in the right place at the right time. The thought comes to me that there are people outside this very minute walking right on by, talking and laughing, not even realizing what bad luck they're having by not stopping in for a jelly doughnut.

After Mama, I help myself to a cake—so fresh my thumb sinks into it. I look over at poor Mama with her mouth full of sweet. A sudden shiver passes through me, and I wonder if a free cake is God's apology for a broken heart.

CHAPTER FOUR

—◆—

"LET'S HURRY," MAMA SAYS as we head toward the hotel. "Manny must be starving. He'll be surprised when he sees what we brought for him." She's holding the doughnut bag in front of her with two hands, as if her mother has told her she will spank her if she drops it.

As soon as we get in the door, the front desk calls us over. "Tomorrow you're out. Right?"

"What?" Mama's eyebrows have snapped to attention. "What are you talking about?"

"Your husband. He gave notice two weeks ago. The suite is rented tomorrow. Be out by noon."

Mama heads for the stairs as if she's going to throw up and is trying to get to the bathroom before the volcano erupts. When we get to our door, her hands are shaking so badly that she can't get the key in the lock.

"Here, let me do that," I say, taking the key out of her hand. I'm not doing much better, but finally the door feels sorry for us and lets us in.

I watch as she walks toward the bed in slow motion, still guarding the precious package with both hands. She turns and sits. Her face is wounded, shattered into pieces like a dropped china cup. The doughnut bag is on her lap now and there will be no spanking. Her arms are wrapped around it. She isn't protecting a doughnut anymore—Manny is in that bag and she's holding on for dear life.

"Here, let me help you lie down," I say quietly so she doesn't jump out of her skin when I touch her. I kneel by the bed so I can take off her shoes. This is going to be harder than I thought. I know there's a way to do this. I just haven't figured it out yet. Her feet stay planted to the floor like someone has glued them there.

My brain starts working so well I surprise myself. "Let's do it this way," I say, tender and sensitive, talking to a scared child.

I'm standing next to the bed, easing the top of her toward the pillow. Her feet are still connected to the floor so she is a square, like one of those tools a carpenter uses. At least now the light has turned green and we can proceed. I bend down and take hold of her ankles. I catch myself before I say *Heave Ho,* because in her condition, there's no telling what will make things even worse than they are already.

I force my brain to pretend it's in a nurse's head. "That's a good girl, Mama. You did a good job."

She is still holding that bag to her front, protecting it with her life. Her dress is wound around wrong, and I can see above where her stockings attach to the garters on her girdle. *Nurses see this kind of thing everyday*, I tell myself. Besides, this is my mother so it's allowed.

Now here is a problem. I should have pulled the spread off the bed while I had the chance. I could have covered her with that. She's all out in the open—a spectacle. Wait a minute! A thought skips through my head. I go over to Manny's side of the bed, loosen the spread, and drag it over her. There!

"Mama, do you want anything?" I ask in a church voice.

"No, Lizzy," she says, closing her eyes. "I'm just going to sleep. Why don't you go to the park? It's too nice to stay inside. I'll be okay."

The thought of going to the park doesn't appeal to me. I'm not in the mood for sunshine and happy families. I go in the kitchenette and empty the percolator into the sink. I watch as the blackness of Mama's life goes down the drain into the sewer. Mine too because I'm attached to her, half because I'm not all the way grown yet and half because she needs me.

Be out by noon.

Out where?

CHAPTER FIVE

THE HAMPER IS FULL. Good. That will give me something to do. Mama is sleeping soundly now. Peace has decorated her face—smooth, gentle. I wonder if the wild look has left her eyes—or is it still there—hiding behind her eyelids, waiting to pounce at me when she opens them?

I reach into her purse for laundry money and find the creamers from the coffee shop. The pink waitress comes into my head. I picture her going home to her husband after her shift is over. He has worked a full day, but there he is in the kitchen. Supper is on the table. He has her slippers waiting. *Sit down honey*, he says to her. *I bought you a present.*

Is this all? she asks, as she throws the gift to the floor and walks out the door, laughing—leaving him there with the look Mama had on her face before she fell asleep.

The world is put together all wrong. How come the Mannys and the pink waitresses end up happy and the Mamas end up hugging jelly doughnuts because that's all they have left? Tears sting my eyes when I think how sadness creeps up and bites you when you're not expecting it.

* * *

I ask the laundry attendant to break a dollar.

"Sure, honey," she says as she rummages around in her pocket for change. "You all alone today? Usually you come in with your mother. She's feeling okay, I hope."

"Oh, yes," I lie. "She's fine. Just thought I would surprise her."

"Well, aren't you the one. I have a daughter about your age. Dirty clothes could be stacked to the ceiling and she wouldn't even notice. The only thing that would get her attention would be if the television set broke and she missed her cartoons."

This is not a question, so I'm not sure what to say. "Huh" with a giggle wrapped around it comes out of my mouth.

"Here you go, sweetie." I watch as she counts the money into my hand. *Her* hands are the color of dark polished wood—like you see in a church—the expensive kind that coaxes you to rub your fingers along it to find out for yourself just how smooth it is.

"Do you need any help?" she asks.

"Help?"

"With the laundry. Do you need any help with your laundry?"

"Oh, no. I'm fine."

If only she hadn't added the part about the laundry. I could have said, Yes, please . . . I do need help. You see, my father is going to marry the harlot and we have to be out tomorrow by noon and my mother has fallen apart. Her eyes are wild and they scare me and she has Manny in a bag and won't let go and there's a dollar and fifteen cents in her purse and the refrigerator is broken so the cream will be spoiled. She will have to take her coffee black. I think I'm drowning. Please help me before I die because of the way I'm feeling inside.

"Okay, honey, I can see you have everything under control. I'll leave you alone. I have some work to do in the office."

Whites in one machine—colors in another. Hot water and bleach for whites. Warm for colors. What's this? Dark blue pants. Manny's pants. Dark blue is not colors. Dark blue is separate—another machine—another quarter. There won't be enough money left for the drying.

Run across the street and get me a doughnut, Lizzy. Make sure it's fresh. You'd better have my change. All of it. You stand right there while I count it. Vonnie, I would like you to meet a friend of mine. This is Sylvia Bushey . . .

The tall green trashcan in the corner is empty. The pants fall to the bottom and make a noise like *There! That's the end of that.*

* * *

The clothes are chasing each other around in the dryer, playing tag, light and dry now like pieces of colored paper being carried by the wind, floating to the bottom and then swooping around to start over again—not a care in the world. The red light is still on and the dryer is mine for ten more minutes. I think of what is waiting for me and I try to hold back time by wishing that the red light would stay on forever.

My eyes focus on Mama's pink blouse and follow it on its journey around the stainless steel drum. It's the one she wears for good, the one she wears when she plays the piano in the hotel, the one that takes me back to her birthday.

"Look, Lizzy," she says when I get home from school carrying the construction-paper card I made for her in art class. "Look at the beautiful blouse Manny gave me for my birthday."

It's the one she bought for herself the week before and hid in the closet while I watched from behind the screen by my bed.

"And look at the beautiful card he gave me. Look here. It's a Hallmark card . . . the best kind. It has real dried pansies and extra pages. And look at this," she says as she turns the card over, puts it close to my face and points to the bottom. "It cost a whole dollar."

"Oh, let me see!" I say with pretend excitement in my voice.

I open the pansies and see how she has signed the card. She didn't think to disguise her handwriting.

Vonnie, I will be yours forever.

All my love, Manny

She doesn't notice the card I'm holding—the one the art teacher let me make while the others were making pinch pots out of clay. Mine doesn't compare to a Hallmark, so I slip it into my notebook and head for the kitchenette to get supper started.

CHAPTER SIX

"HEY, KID! WAIT UP." Manny and the harlot catch up to me outside our hotel. "Give this to Vonnie, will you?" He's standing there holding out an envelope. Finally, a light bulb goes on in his head that tells him my hands are busy holding a basket of clothes. He sticks the envelope under my chin and expects me to clamp onto it like I'm playing pass the orange.

"She can't carry it like that, Manny."

He has found himself a genius! The harlot reaches under my chin and takes the envelope. She tucks it into the laundry basket beside the towels.

"My name is Sylvia Bushey. Happy to meet you. Manny here has told me all about you."

The genius is standing there with her hand out, expecting me to shake it.

It's amazing what daylight does to someone who's trying to be something she isn't. The harlot doesn't look anything like last night. Last night, the spotlight was on Mama. The harlot was protected by the shadows. Today, the sun is telling it the way it is.

It's easy to see that Manny has found a perfect match. This is the first time I've seen black hair with blond roots. It's usually the other way around—this one is hard to figure. Mama says it's all right to use just a hint of makeup as long as it looks natural. The harlot doesn't hint around about her makeup, and there's nothing natural about it unless she was born with the wrong color foundation that stops at her chin, topped off by raccoon eyes with eyelashes that look as if they've grown fur. The royal blue dress she's wearing is shiny and has fake jewels across the top. It makes you wonder why anyone would take the time to make something that ugly. One of the jewels has fallen off, and the glue that used to hold it on looks like a blob of toothpaste. For a second, before you realize what you're looking at, you give her credit for brushing her teeth. She has done a good job of matching the color on her eyelids to the dress, but it must be yesterday's because it has settled into the creases, and it looks more like stripes than shadow. I am enjoying this. I like how God pops up once in a while and gives you a present. I wish Mama could see this.

"Tell your mother to sign those papers and bring them down to me," Manny says. "I'll be at the bar all night. And kid, Sylvia and I are going to be away for a few weeks, so we'll see you when we get back. Don't take any wooden nickels while we're gone."

The harlot thinks that's the funniest thing she's ever heard. Now I'm absolutely positive I'm never going to have kids. With my luck, my baby would be born stupid with greasy hair and a mustache.

Manny doesn't think of it, so Sylvia holds the door for me. "Nice to make your acquaintance," she says as I walk away.

"Hey, kid! You didn't happen to find my good pants in the hamper, did you?" Manny says around the toothpick he has parked at the side of his mouth.

"Your good pants? What do they look like?"

"They're brand new, navy blue. I bought them for a special occasion."

I am loving this! Thank you, God. "No, I didn't see them. If I find them, I'll bring them down."

* * *

I hear water running in the bathroom. I sit in the chair by the window not knowing what to expect. The doughnut bag is on the night stand next to *Passion Before Midnight.* At least it's not sitting on Manny's pillow. Putting the laundry away seems like a waste of time. *Be out by noon* is almost here. The clothes will be easier to pack if they're in one place—folded and ready.

Mama comes out of the bathroom with her head down, embarrassed. How do I go about this? Start out slow and easy. "Did you have a good nap?" I ask with fake cheerfulness in my voice.

"Yes, thank you," she says, not missing a beat, but still looking at the floor. "I feel much better. I shouldn't have acted so silly. I remember now . . . Manny told me we were moving. I just forgot."

Mama gets an A-plus for lying. Being a grown-up woman is too complicated. I don't want to be one—ever! But, maybe it's not the grown-up woman part that is complicated. I think it's men that mess everything up. That's not a problem. I just won't get one. This is something important to be stored in a safe place in my mind and remembered. There, now I feel better.

Her head is still down. I'll try something else. "I did the laundry while you were sleeping, Mama." Okay, now she's looking at me. This is a safe place.

"That was so nice of you. Here, let me put it away."

I remember the letter. I'd better tell her before she sees it. "Manny asked me to give you this envelope."

The wild eyes flash and her face reddens—a failure—something to be pitied. "Oh . . . this must be the insurance policy he told me about," she says, grabbing it away from me. Sadness has crept over her face again. She's holding her future in her hand—a live frightening thing.

"He asked me to tell you to sign it and take it down to him." I don't know what to do or where to look, so I pick invisible lint off my blouse.

She stands for a time saying nothing and then she comes back from her thoughts. "I'll do that right now," she says, heading for the door—slow motion again.

"Do you want me to come with you? Mama? Do you want me to come with you?"

The door closes, but it doesn't latch, and I can hear heavy feet going toward the stairs.

There's only time enough for me to get a drink of water and go to the bathroom before I hear the footsteps coming back. They're slow and sad so she didn't get what she was hoping for. This time the begging didn't work. He didn't give her time to list the reasons he should stay. This harlot has a different name, but she's the same as all the others. This one has won the game. But, Mama . . . why can't you see? She's gotten the booby prize. You're worth so much more. Why don't you know that? Didn't anybody ever tell you? You should be glad to be rid of him. I am. I try not to let the feather I feel in my heart come to the surface. I would feel too guilty when she's down so low. Tomorrow—out by noon. Any place will be better than this.

The footsteps stop before they get to our door. I hear a coin fall into the pay phone down the hall and then Mama's voice. "I'd like to make a collect call to Ridgewood, New York, Mr. Frank Warner, Mason Street. I'm sorry, but I've forgotten the number. Yes, I'll hold. Thank you. Hello, Daddy? It's Veronica. Veronica, Daddy. I'm calling from Phoenix. Phoenix! Can you hear me now? I know it has . . . too long. I'm sorry. I'd like to come home for a visit. I want you and Mommy to meet Lizzy. Lizzy. My daughter. Tomorrow. We'll be leaving tomorrow on the bus. I don't know . . . maybe a week or two . . . I don't know. No, he won't be coming. He has to work. It will just be the two of us. There's something I have to ask you. There's been a mix-up at the bank. Do you think you could wire some money? Just enough to get us home. I'll pay you back as soon as the bank clears things up. We'll see you in a few days. And Daddy . . . thank you."

Oh, my heart—the feather has turned into eagles' wings flapping so hard they're about to carry me away. Ridgewood, New York! In a few days! Were my ears playing tricks on me? We're going to Ridgewood, New York! We'll leave Manny here and I'll help Mama find a new husband, one who will appreciate her, one who wants to be somebody's father. My heart is ready to burst clear out of my body. Mama has a mother and a father. She never said anything about them. Maybe she was keeping them a secret for a giant surprise—this one!

I get away from the door, cross the room in a breath to let her have the fun of breaking the news to me. I'm sitting near the window looking out. My face says I don't suspect a thing.

"Are you hungry?" she asks when she comes into the room. Her voice is weak, as if her batteries are running low. "I'll heat up some soup. We're out of bread so we'll have to have crackers."

Soup and crackers? That's not the surprise! I'm ready. Let me have it! "Soup and crackers sounds good."

"Do you have any library books you haven't returned?"

Here it comes—she's warming up. "No, Mama . . . I took them all back."

"That's good."

If she's trying to kill me, she's doing a good job.

"I have an errand I have to do this afternoon, Lizzy. You can come with me or you can stay here. Whatever you want."

Now, this is something I can grab hold of. "What kind of errand?"

"I have to walk down to Western Union."

This is no help. I don't know what Western Union is. The bus station, maybe? "Why do you have to walk down to Western Union?"

"I have to pick up something."

I am so close to dead, they might as well get out the shovel. "What do you have to pick up?"

"Some money. My father is sending us some money."

Come on. Come on. You can tell me. "Why is he sending us money?" If this doesn't do it, I'm going to tell *her* that we're going to Ridgewood, New York—on a bus—tomorrow.

"He called and asked if we would visit him."

I'm getting tired of these lies. Two can play at this game. She had her chance. Now it's my turn. "Oh really?"

"I thought you'd be excited."

I was . . . about two hours ago. "Where does he live?"

"Ridgewood. Ridgewood, New York."

"That's awfully far. How will we get there?"

"On a bus."

"We're going to take a bus? Oh . . . I see. When is all of this going to take place?"

"Tomorrow. We'll leave tomorrow."

"What about Manny?" That one slipped out. I wish I could take it back. Now I feel terrible. Sometimes I'm so evil I don't recognize myself.

"Manny won't be coming. He has to stay here to work."

I have to try to make it up to her. "This sounds like fun, Mama. I can't wait! You take it easy. I'll fix lunch and then we'll walk to Western Union."

The eagles are back in my heart. I hope the bus has those tip-back seats because I'm not going to sleep a wink tonight!

CHAPTER SEVEN

MAMA AND I ARE AT the bus station in Albany waiting for her father to pick us up. She's trying to be nice, but I know she's still mad at me because I ate Manny. The second day we were on the road, she fell asleep with the doughnut bag on her lap. I was sick of looking at it and I was so hungry that the evil side of me came out. When she woke up, I made like I didn't know what she was talking about when she asked about the crime.

"I have no idea what happened to it," I say, unable to look her in the eye. "Maybe it fell on the floor. Why don't you look down there?"

"Lizzy, you have sugar all over your face. Why are you lying to me?"

Because I learned from an expert, that's why! "I'm sorry I lied. I was just so hungry." Let's see what she comes up with for this one. "Why were you keeping that doughnut anyway? It was stale."

"I was saving it for my father. He loves jelly doughnuts."

She's good. The way she lies without a hitch—it's as if she has buckets of them stored away in her head. Any time she needs one, she dips into a bucket, and a lie comes flowing out her mouth like water.

* * *

I could be in "Ripley's Believe It or Not!" I have never been in a car before. When Mama's father drives into the parking lot, my eyes must look like Little Orphan Annie's. This is not just a car—this is a Cadillac! Why didn't Mama tell me he's rich?

Wait just a minute. The man getting out of that car doesn't look like a Cadillac person. He's just regular. He's coming toward us, and he's getting less Cadillac with every step. He has a tall knobbly body, pointy elbows, and long bony hands with rivers of giant veins running down them. The skin on his face is thin and spotty, and the bones of his cheeks are trying to push their way through it. He's wearing gray pants the same color as his hair, the handyman kind with a belt that's pulled too tight, and his white socks make the brown of his shoes look even darker. He has Mama's eyes, so blue and friendly it's hard not to stare at them.

"Hello, Daddy," Mama says, standing there with her hand out.

"Hello, Veronica. How have you been?"

They're shaking hands. This isn't like in the movies. I don't know what to do, so I stare at my feet.

"Daddy, this is Lizzy."

My turn!

"Lizzy, this is my father. Your grandfather Warner."

My *grandfather*. Now, this is something I haven't thought about. I roll the words around in my head. They feel good. He's holding out his hand. He treats me just like I'm his daughter. *Wake up, Lizzy*, I tell myself. I wipe my hand on my dress just in case and then I shake my grandfather's hand. It's dry and cool. I don't care if he doesn't match his car. He's my grandfather.

"Why, Lizzy," he says, patting my head, "you're as pretty as an Adirondack autumn. Just like your mother when she was your age."

My heart is overflowing with happiness. I don't know what an Adirondack autumn is, but he said I was pretty. Nobody has ever said *that* before.

* * *

I am in the lap of luxury. I have the whole back seat of a Cadillac to myself. Mama is sitting up front with her father—my grandfather—and they're talking about baseball. She's throwing names around like she knows what she's talking about—Roger Maris, Yogi Berra, Mickey Mantle. This is a Mama I don't know. This is a new and improved Mama. The two of them are laughing and talking like they're in a race to the finish line. This is Mama when Manny McMann is not in her head. This is Mama when she's with someone who thought she was as pretty as an Adirondack autumn when she was my age.

I'm looking at the back of my grandfather's head and the little hairs on his neck and I'm trying to decide what to call him. I thought about asking him, but this is a big decision and I want to make it myself. Grandfather doesn't fit. Grandfather sounds cold. It's for castles and soap operas where people live in mansions. Gramps? No, that's wrong. It sounds too much like cramps. Grandpa is nice. It fits him, it feels good in my head. I'll have to find out what he thinks. Here goes, I'm going to jump right in and see what happens.

"Grandpa, how far is it to Ridgewood?"

"About a hundred and fifty miles. Almost to the Canadian border."

Okay, that worked. I'll try it one more time just to make sure he heard me right. "Why didn't we just keep taking the bus, Grandpa?" This is starting to feel comfortable.

"Oh . . . I wanted a little time by myself with the two of you before we get home."

"How *is* Mommy, Daddy?" Mama says the words like her tongue has turned to ice.

"She's the same. I think it's going to be the Yanks against the Giants in the series this year. What do you think?"

* * *

"Lizzy, those are the Adirondacks."

My grandpa is calling me. I can't believe I fell asleep and missed part of my Cadillac ride. "Where are they? Show me."

"Over there, those big beautiful mountains. That one right in front of us is Whiteface. In the winter, people come from all over the world to ski down that mountain."

It looks majestic, like it's the king of all the other peaks nearby, as if God put it there to watch over them like a doting parent. You can see the ski trails looking like the veins on my grandfather's hands.

"Grandpa, what does an Adirondack autumn look like?"

"Oh, my goodness," he says with a sigh, "it's the most beautiful sight you could ever imagine. I wish you could stay long enough to see one. You would never forget it as long as you live. The trees turn colors so bright and vivid it almost hurts your eyes to look at them. Every year it's as if God gets out his prettiest paints and decorates the leaves like he's getting them ready to go to a party. It takes your breath away."

If happiness could kill a person, I would fall over dead right here in the back seat of this Cadillac.

* * *

"Everything looks so different, Daddy," Mama says, swiveling her head so she doesn't miss anything. "When did they build that shopping center?"

A sign has just told us that we are entering Ridgewood, New York—population thirty thousand, home of the Ridgewood Air Force Base—and that we should enjoy our stay.

"A lot of things have changed," Grandpa says, sounding as if the sun has set on his mood. "These young kids that are running the city seem to think that bigger means better."

"How's your business doing?" Mama asks.

"Well . . . that's another story." He grips the steering wheel tighter and I can see the bones of his knuckles right through his skin. "Since the chains have come in, they're trying to choke the life out of the little guys and they're doing a pretty good job of it. I still have some loyal customers who want their meat cut to order and their groceries delivered, but I don't know how long it'll last. I just can't compete with the big stores' prices. I've been thinking a lot lately about retiring, but I don't know what I'd do all day at home."

"What does Mommy think of that?" Mama asks, staring straight ahead.

"I haven't found the right time to bring it up. Here we are ladies. Home Sweet Home."

So this is it. It doesn't pay to wrack your brain trying to picture something before you've seen it with your own eyes. As soon as I stepped into this car, I started imagining the house that went with it. A Cadillac goes with a big brick house with white pillars and a swimming pool like the ones in the movies. The house that goes with this one is small. It's made of gray wood and there are no pillars. It's pretty and neat, but this is not what I expected. The sun is shining on its smooth green lawn and there are flower boxes under the windows. This house is friendly, like my grandpa.

A pretty gray-haired woman is sitting on the porch in a rocking chair watching us. I don't have to try out names for her. Grandma goes with Grandpa. I'm all set. The words are in my mind and ready to go. When the time comes, I'll wait until she hugs me and then I'll say, *Hello, Grandma . . . I'm so happy to meet you.* It surprises me when a picture of the witch's house in *Hansel and Gretel* comes into my head. Where did that come from? Maybe it's just because her house is small too.

Grandma does not get out of her chair when we climb the stairs to the porch. She keeps rocking and doesn't look at us. Instead, she stares straight ahead at the cars going by on the street like she's counting them and doesn't want to lose her place.

"Well, Veronica," she says, still counting cars, "I see you finally came crawling home. What's the problem? Did Romeo trade you in on a new model? I told you that would happen." When she turns her head to look at my mother, the folds on her neck remind me of chicken skin—all loose and quivery. "I can't say I blame him. Look how you've let yourself go. How do you expect to hold onto a man, looking like that? If you'd listened to me, you wouldn't be in this mess."

Her words come out all sing-songy, and while she's saying *this mess*, she tilts her head in my direction to make it clear that I'm the mess she's talking about. Her face has a *so there* look on it, and my mother's face has turned to stone. The new and improved Mama—the talking and laughing one who knows all about baseball has disappeared—a wisp of smoke blown away by my grandmother's words.

"I'll just get these bags inside," Grandpa says, not looking at anybody. The spell is broken. Now it's clear where the witch's house came from. My mind must have known ahead of time who lived here. Mama follows my grandfather and I follow her.

This must be a mistake. The inside of this house doesn't go with sunshine and flower boxes and a smooth green lawn. It goes with sadness and brown. The smell hits me in the face like a slap, and then it becomes a shroud and wraps itself around me. It's mothballs and cabbage and Vicks and old grease. It's unwashed curtains and Evening in Paris perfume. I hold my breath as long as I can to keep it from becoming part of me. But in the end, it wins and forces its way into my body like a prowler sneaking in a window and leaving its dirty fingerprints on my insides.

This house is like April Fool's Day or a practical joke, the kind where somebody gives you a gift wrapped in flowered paper tied with a beautiful bow and you expect to find something wonderful. But when you open it, there it is. A dead rat.

A dark, heavy feeling fills the core of me when I think about my mother growing up in this house with her mother who's standing behind me making the hairs on the back of my neck stand on end—a woman whose heart is locked from the inside.

"Where's my piano, Mommy?" Mama asks with panic in her voice. Her mouth is hanging open and she's staring at a light shape on the soiled wallpaper that points out where the missing piano used to be. A photograph of a dead child on display for all to see.

"I sold it when I heard you were coming back." The words slither out of her mouth full of venom. "Where did you think I was going to get the money to feed you? You run off with that snake in the grass and then turn up like a bad penny and expect everything to be the same as when you left." She takes a rumpled handkerchief from her apron pocket and slides it across her dry nose. "You made your bed when you left with him, and now you can sleep in it." She says the word *him* like it makes her sick to her stomach. "Besides, I had to make a place for *her* to sleep. You can bring the cot down from the attic. Just make sure it's put away before I come downstairs in the morning."

My breath tumbles out of me and I feel an emptiness where my heart is supposed to be. I'm the *her* she's talking about because she tilted her head my way again to make sure Mama got her point, but she still hasn't looked at me or spoken to me. I can see that as far as my grandmother is concerned, Mama ran away with one snake and brought another one home with her.

"I thought Lizzy and I would be sleeping in my room," Mama whines.

"What room are you talking about, Veronica? This isn't your house. You don't have a room here. You're a grown woman. You're supposed to have your own house." She sniffs and clears her throat. "If you'd listened to me, you'd be married to that

nice Tommy Brand and you'd be living on Oakwood Avenue in
a new split-level with an in-ground pool. He married the Larson
girl, you know, right after you left. She knew a good thing when
she saw it, and look where she is now. And look at you."

"I didn't love Tommy Brand, Mommy." Mama's eyes are
drilling a hole in the floor and I'm wishing I could fall into it
and disappear. It's worse for her having me here. If she were
alone, she could pack the ugly words away in the part of her
mind where she stores such things and leave them there—pretend
that she never heard them, lie about them. Because I'm hearing them too, they're on display, an embarrassment, like when
somebody opens the door on you when you're in the bathroom.
You try to cover yourself, but it's too late, your secret is already
in their head. If my grandmother's meanness could turn into
something you could see, it would be dark, murky quicksand
that slowly pulls anyone who gets too close to it into its depths
and suffocates him.

"Well *la-di-da*, Veronica," my grandmother says, rocking her
head back and forth like the pendulum on a clock. "Now you
can see how long love lasts and where it gets you. You'll be the
laughing stock of Ridgewood. Poor Veronica, they'll say. Got
herself pregnant and ran off with a useless nobody and then
came crawling back when he threw her away." She looks at me
for the first time, and while her eyes stay locked on mine she
says, "Was *this* worth throwing your life away and breaking
your father's heart?"

*Tell her I was worth it, Mama. Tell her I was worth whatever it
was you had to do.* Her silence satisfies my grandmother and she
lets go of my eyes and aims her disapproval back at my mother.
"The room where you used to sleep is your father's now. You'll be
sleeping on the davenport. Beggars can't be choosers. You should
be grateful that we're taking you in." I can tell by the look on her
face that she is enjoying what she's doing to my mother.

I can see my grandfather through the window. He's in the
front yard trimming a hedge that doesn't need to be trimmed.

A mouse staying out of the cat's way, willing to let the weaker mouse get eaten.

I feel terrible for Mama. I know how disappointed she is about her piano. She told me how much she loved it while we were on the bus. "Lizzy, just wait until you see it," she said with excitement in her voice. "It's so beautiful. It's a Baldwin. My grandfather gave it to me on my seventh birthday. Then he paid for my piano lessons with Miss Lucy Simpson until I graduated from high school, just before he died. I was her prize pupil you know."

This is the millionth time she's told me about the prize pupil part, but I didn't know about the Baldwin that makes her face light up like a sunny day when she talks about it.

"Mommy and Daddy are keeping it for me until we have a house of our own. Then I'll teach you how to play and maybe even give music lessons to make extra money."

I'm not the least bit disappointed about not learning how to play the piano. I'm more the drums type or maybe the trumpet like Herb Alpert. I feel sorry for Mama in an impatient way. I wish she would realize that she's a grown woman and stop calling her mother Mommy. I'm going to have to work on that one.

We're stuck here—Mama and I—stray dogs begging for scraps. I know that as well as everybody else in this house. This isn't a visit. This is a prison sentence without a trial. My grandmother had forever to ruin my mother, and I'm sure that she's counting on me to be her next victim. What she doesn't realize is that I am *not* my mother. I am Lizzy McMann. I watched Manny beat Mama down for as long as I can remember and I have made a promise to myself. Nobody will ever do that to me. It's going to take a lot more than a mean old woman to conquer me. She's met her match. Bring her on.

CHAPTER EIGHT

I AM SO GLAD THAT SCHOOL has started. All I did all summer was work on the lawn with my grandpa to stay out of my grandmother's way. I'm now an expert at digging dandelions, spreading fertilizer, and sharpening lawn mower blades. If Ridgewood had a best-looking lawn contest, we would win it without even trying. Ours is the only house on the block that gets its lawn mowed every day.

My grandmother hasn't started in on me yet. She's still chipping away at my mother. Mama just stands there and takes it like she did with Manny. If she were a dog, her ears would be down and her tail would be tucked between her legs. I wonder why Grandpa doesn't step in and stop her, but he must have his reasons. I haven't been here long enough to figure out what they are.

I'm trying to find a way to help Mama get a backbone. You would think in a house where it's three against one that the three would win. In this house, it doesn't work that way. My grandmother is like those gigantic hickory nuts you get at Christmas. You need a hammer to open them, and sometimes even that doesn't work, so you put it back in the bowl and try another kind before you end up smashing your fingers.

My school is just down the street from our house, so I don't
have to take the bus like I did in Phoenix. It's part of the Ridgewood Teachers' College. We are guinea pigs. The college students practice on us before they're let loose to teach in regular
schools. They have to observe the real teacher for a few weeks
before they start, so we have time to learn some stuff before
they get hold of us.

I'm in the seventh grade. The first day I walked into my
classroom, I nearly fainted when I found out that my teacher is
a man. I thought I would have to wait for high school before I
got one. His name is Mr. Stephens, and I hope that if he has any
kids, they know how lucky they are to have him for a father. He
knew every one of our names by the end of the very first day,
and I don't think he would yell at anyone if his life depended on
it. He's not dying to catch you being wrong like most teachers.
He's just the opposite. If you give a dumb answer to a question,
he will say with seriousness on his face, "That was a good try,
but it's not exactly what I was looking for. You think about it
a little more and I'll come back to you." But of course, out of
pure courtesy, he does not go back because he knows that the
kid will be just as dumb the second time around. That kind of
thing leaves you with the feeling you will do anything you can
to please this man. He's on your side.

My last year's teacher only knew the names of the geniuses
and the really stupid ones. I'm high average and I behave myself,
so I just got pointed at when she wanted me to do something.
It made her so happy when somebody messed up, you would
think she had won first place in the Miss America contest,
which would have never happened in a million years because
her looks matched her personality. She would do well to take a
whole chapter out of Mr. Stephens' book.

The girl who sits next to me is a copying fool. Her father
is our gym teacher, and he's so drop-dead handsome that the
boy-crazy girls have coronaries every time they see him. Because
of that, she thinks she owns the school and can get away with

murder. She even copies things a two-year-old could do with one eye closed and her hands tied behind her back. She copies like Mama lies. Half the time I don't think she even knows she's doing it. Plus, I think she's a little low in the brains department. The smartest kid in our class sits on the other side of her, but she copies from me anyway. One of these days she'll make a mistake and copy my name onto her paper and the jig will be up. The teacher will wonder why there are two Lizzy McMann papers and no Madeline Brand. I'll take the high road and keep my mouth shut. Our teacher is smart. He'll figure it out.

I'm taking my time making friends. As far as I can see, everybody is already spoken for except Madeline Brand, and she's not my type. Besides being a copying fool, she still wears her hair in ringlets. She brings her doll to school and sits it on her seat next to her and talks to it. I know I'm no prize, but I can do better than that. I'm the one on the outside looking in, so I have to be patient and hope they come to me.

I'm not going to make the same mistake I did in Phoenix. That was fourth grade, when we moved there from Miami right after Christmas. The girl who sat next to me invited me home for supper the very first day. That should have clued me in right off the bat. She latched onto me like a bloodsucker and wouldn't let go. How was I to know that she was the class nose-picker and the biggest tattletale in the whole school? It doesn't pay to make snap decisions. Who you choose to be your friends can determine your destiny, so I'm not taking any chances. I'm going to learn from my mistakes.

CHAPTER NINE

MAMA HAS GOTTEN A JOB at a drugstore downtown. She applied for the cosmetics position, but since she's not the cosmetics type, they made her a waitress and put her behind the luncheonette counter. She has a uniform like the pink waitress in Phoenix, only hers is mint green and it has all its buttons. The head thing she has to wear is white with ruffles that match the apron. I showed her how to fluff her hair around the bobby pins so that nobody would even know they're there. She had to borrow money from Grandpa behind my grandmother's back to buy white nurse's shoes with crepe soles to finish off her outfit.

"Lizzy, I never thought my life would turn out like this," she tells me her first day on the job. It's Saturday and I'm walking her to work because she's scared to go alone. Her uniform is too short and the skin on her legs above her knee-hi stockings reminds me of the blue cheese in the A&P dairy section, but as long as she stays straight up, it doesn't show.

"I had such big plans," she tells me as she stares down toward the sidewalk at the new shoes. "I was going to be a famous piano player like Liberace."

I have to be careful when she starts talking like this, because if I say what's in my head, I could turn into my grandmother without even trying. "Don't worry, Mama," I say. "You just wait. You *will* be as famous as Liberace some day." The lie winds itself around my tongue and then lets go and falls out of my mouth as free and easy as air.

"Do you really think so?" she asks with a look of desperation in her eyes.

"Of course I do."

"I'm just glad Manny can't see me in this uniform," she says, giving the apron a twist to center it over her stomach, which has gotten even bigger since my grandmother started chewing on her. "And I'm going to be so embarrassed if I have to wait on my friends from high school."

Now this is something I haven't thought about before. Mama's having friends is a new idea for my brain to toss around. For as long as I've known her, she's had only Manny and me—mostly just me. Trying to picture her with friends is like looking at a blank piece of paper and hoping something will appear out of nowhere. Nothing does because there isn't anything to work with.

"What friends are those?" I ask.

"Bertie mostly . . . and Martha." She looks sad, but her eyes are busy tending to something else. The something else looks as if it could be hope, only it has a cover on it, like when you think something good might be going to happen but you don't want to put too much into it, because if you do, you'll ruin it. So you bury it just under the surface where it's safe, but where you can get to it quickly. Just in case.

"Who's Bertie, Mama?"

She doesn't answer. She's gone somewhere else—back to high school, I think, with Bertie mostly and Martha.

A picture comes into my mind of two high school girls—pretty and popular, dressed in wool pleated skirts and cashmere sweater sets, talking and laughing—walking home from school, or maybe to a party. Behind them is Mama in her waitress uniform with her head down and the sadness on her face. "Come on, Veronica," one of them calls to her. "You're going to make us late!" The stiff white shoes with the crepe soles hurry noiselessly to catch up with the two pairs of Bass Weejuns that are making smart clapping noises on the sidewalk. There isn't enough room for three abreast, so Mama walks behind like an afterthought.

"Well, this is it. Major's Drugstore." She has stopped and is staring at the double doors in front of her. She's forgotten about the apron and it's traveled halfway around her waist.

"Here, let me fix that for you," I say, yanking it back to its proper place. "Are you going to be okay? Do you want me to go in with you?"

"No. I have to do this myself. You go on home now. I'll be fine. I'll see you at five. And Lizzy . . . try to stay out of Mommy's way. She's not feeling well today."

"I will," I say as I walk away thinking how Mama always makes excuses for my grandmother's meanness. It's a mystery to me why anybody would want to go through life raining on everybody else's mood. She's a gob of spit in a pitcher of lemonade.

CHAPTER TEN

———————

I'M ALMOST HOME, just down the street from my house when I hear a voice say, "Hey, kid!" Manny comes into my head, but the voice that goes with the words is wrong for him. The house I'm walking by belongs to a girl who goes to my school, an eighth grader who looks like Natalie Wood. In school, she's always by herself. She's so pretty that I think the other girls are too jealous to be around her. Sometimes when I pass by her house, she is sitting on her porch and she looks me over as if she's checking to see if her rash has gone away. Today is different. She is not on the porch and she's talking to me, only I can't see her.

"Hey, kid. Want a drag?"

I stop and look over at the house. Nothing. She's playing a joke on me.

"I'm up here. Do you want a drag?"

Now I see where she is. She's in an upstairs window with her face just inside the screen. A mystery. She's holding a cigarette and pointing to it.

"Oh. Sure," I say before my brain has a chance to interfere.

This is not just *anybody* inviting me in for a cigarette. This is an eighth grader. One who looks like Natalie Wood and smokes. A big deal. I give her a look that tells her I don't know what to do next, so she says to walk in the front door and go up the stairs. Nobody's home. It's okay.

"Oh," I say, smiling, and then my feet get a mind of their own and take me toward the front door and into the house. This is when it would be nice to be able to put your life in reverse and take the other path, like if somebody tells you to jump off a cliff and you do. The minute you take the first step, you wish you could go back and say, "No, thanks."

One thing I know for sure is that this family is rich. I can tell that right off the bat. First of all, their front door has one of those wide brass strips at the bottom that costs extra, but is only for show. I'm not letting myself be fooled by that because of my grandpa's Cadillac, but when I open the door and go into the living room, here is the proof. A grand piano, a Steinway, all but filling up the room.

I know about Steinways, because every time one comes on TV, Mama nearly has a heart attack telling me how expensive they are and how only rich people like Liberace can afford them. When the cameraman zooms in to get a shot of Liberace's rings, she points and says, "Look, Lizzy, it even says it right there. Can you see it?" One of these days, my evilness will seep out and I will say something smart-alecky about how I would have to be blind not to be able to see it and how I don't give a gnat's ass about it anyway. But then I will have to clean up the pieces after she falls apart because of my sass and my dirty mouth.

"Come on up," the voice says from the top of the stairs.

"Oh, okay," I hear myself say in a tape recorder voice—like when you hear yourself for the first time and you don't believe it's you because you couldn't possibly sound like that much of a dope.

She's at the top of the stairs with one arm hugging her waist and the other in a movie star pose holding the cigarette near her cheek. She's wearing a green T-shirt and jean shorts and her legs are still tan from the summer. When I get almost there, I see her bare feet with bright red nail polish on her toes. The

second toe on her right foot has a silver ring on it just like a
model in a magazine.

"You made it okay, I see," she says when I reach the top step.

If I had said something that dumb, I'd be beating myself over
the head. Hearing it come out of her mouth is a whole other
story. Coming from her it sounds like *How do you do. I'm so
happy to meet you.*

"My room's down here," she says, leading the way.

Well, this is not what I expected. This is just an ordinary
room, plus it looks as if it blew up and nobody bothered to
clean up the mess. I'm feeling better already. I was worried that
I wouldn't know how to act in Natalie Wood's bedroom.

"Just shove those clothes on the floor. You can sit there."
She's talking about a pile of dirty laundry, even underwear, on
her bed near where I'm standing.

"Oh, that's okay," I say. "I'll just push them over."

She shrugs her shoulders and says, "Whatever floats your
boat."

Now that's one I've never heard before. I'll have to remember it.

She sits down on the other side of the bed. It's the old-fashioned kind with the square canopy top, only this one doesn't
have the cloth part, just the wood. She uses that as a closet and
has piled layers of clothes on it, the best kind, even Danskin tops
and reversible Pendelton pleated wool skirts that cost seventy-five
dollars apiece and the matching wool sweaters. Mock turtleneck.
I think she couldn't make up her mind, so she bought them all.
Even that isn't the grand finale. Her closet is open and so full
of blouses and blazers and more skirts it looks as if it has eaten
too much and is about to explode.

"So, what's your name?" she asks as she shakes a pack of
Newport menthols in my direction like she's sprinkling salt on
a plate of French fries. I'm about to be found out. I think of the
attic at home where I could be alone and hidden and I wouldn't
be wearing my fear on my face and I wouldn't have to smoke

my first cigarette in front of Natalie Wood. If only I could go back and take the other path.

"Are you going to take one or not?" she asks with impatience in her voice.

"Oh, sure. Thanks." It looks so fresh and clean, like a new white pencil that hasn't been sharpened yet. I would like to keep it that way and not ruin it. And not make a fool of myself in the bargain.

"Here you go," she says, holding a Bic in front of my face and snapping the top so the flame jumps out like a jack-in-the-box. I have stepped off the cliff. There's no turning back now and there's nothing to grab hold of to save myself.

"Hold onto my hand." Her voice has a chuckle in it. "You're shaking like a leaf. Is this your first cigarette? Come on. Hold onto my hand. You'll never get it lighted like that."

I cup my hand over hers and guide the lighter toward my mouth like I've seen them do in the movies. I watch as the new pencil is sharpened and the inside is exposed never to be the same again. *I* will never be the same again either, because when my hand touches hers, the deepest most private part of my body becomes the Fourth of July full of sparklers and firecrackers and I want this feeling, whatever it is, to go on forever.

"That's enough! You're going to start a goddamn fire!"

Coming out of *her* mouth, the swearword sounds as if it has been cleaned and polished. There are separate rules for people who look like her. When Manny says that word, it comes out sounding like his smell. You have to wonder about the fairness of things like that.

"Oh, sorry," I say as I let go of her hand.

"This *is* your first cigarette. I thought so. Well, don't inhale then. I don't want you puking all over the place. That's what I did when I had my first one. I hurled my guts all over my mother's brand new kitchen carpet."

I am definitely in over my head. I don't know how to talk to this girl. This girl who makes my insides race with a newness

I don't understand. Whatever I say is going to make me sound like an idiot and that's the last thing I want.

"You haven't told me your name yet," she says, pulling her hair back into a ponytail and then letting it go. "Mine's Eva. Eva Singer. I'm Jewish."

She adds the Jewish part like she's telling me she's a dentist or a lawyer. I should have known she'd be special in the religion department too. Nothing about this girl is ordinary.

"I'm Elizabeth McMann," I say, leaving out the Baptist part.

"You don't look like an Elizabeth," she says, tilting her head and examining my face under a microscope.

"You look more like a Beth. Is it okay with you if I call you Beth?"

"Sure," I tell her. "Beth is fine." It's more than fine. When it comes out of her mouth, it sounds like a whisper. A secret between just the two of us.

"Here, let me have that," she says, taking the cigarette out of my hand. "I can tell you don't want it. I don't really smoke either. These are my mother's cigarettes. I just used them as an excuse to meet you."

Right here, I'm so flabbergasted I could fall on the floor and faint dead away. I could die this very minute with my face buried in Eva Singer's dirty laundry and I wouldn't mind it one little bit. In fact, I would have a smile on my face. The way she said the part about wanting to meet me, I knew she meant it true as anything.

This is when you have to believe that there are certain directions set out for just you to follow, like in a dress pattern. If you ignore them and try to put your life together yourself, you will end up wrong.

I hear the toilet flush and I know the cigarettes Eva Singer used to meet me are following each other down the drain. I know too that how I feel about this girl is a sin, but I don't know how to stop it. It would be like trying to keep the rain from falling or the sun from shining. I wonder if these feelings inside of me are a part of the directions that have been set out for just me to follow, and if I ignore them or try to make them disappear, my life will turn out wrong. How can I know the answer when the thought of what has happened to me is so wonderful and yet so evil? Still, I'm glad I didn't take the other path, the safe one, because this one seems so right for me.

"Where did you live before you moved here?" she asks when she comes back into the room and drops down on the bed.

"Who? Me?" Well, now I've done it. Who else could she mean? I'm such a moron.

"Yeah. Where did you live before here?"

"Phoenix. I lived in Phoenix."

"Where's that?"

I have to be careful here. Maybe this is a joke or a trick question. No, I can tell by her face that she's serious.

"Arizona. Phoenix is in Arizona."

"Oh. I thought so."

This doesn't mean anything. I didn't know where Ridgewood was before I moved here.

"I had never heard of Ridgewood," I tell her to take some of the pressure off. "When my mother told me we were moving here, I thought she was making it up. I made her show me on a map that this place really existed. I'm so bad at geography that if I was in a contest, they'd kick me out before it even started."

All right. Now I've overdone it. She's looking at me and wondering why she's gotten herself mixed up with such a nit-wit. The next thing I know she'll be showing me the door and slamming it behind me.

"Yeah, me too," she says. "I have trouble in school, especially reading. I see everything all scrambled up, sometimes even backward. I have to go to special classes. My parents think it's their fault, something they did before I was born, so they buy me things to make up for it."

I smile, but don't know where to look or what to say. This girl, this Eva Singer, has just opened herself up to me in a way I never could with anybody. She has thrown a burning log in my lap and now she's waiting to see what I'm going to do with it.

"You have really pretty things," I say, making my eyes travel around her room like the pointer Mr. Stephens uses when he's showing us something on a map.

"You can borrow this stuff any time you want," she says. "We're about the same size. Did anybody ever tell you that you look like Audrey Hepburn?"

Well, now, this just goes to show that you'd better be ready for anything. Sometimes God gets it into his head to give you a bonus when you're not expecting it and you say to yourself, now what did I do to deserve this? Like when you get a gold star on a school paper that you didn't put much effort into. I think it's His way of telling us not to give up. Something good might be just around the next corner.

"Audrey Hepburn! Are you kidding?" I'm trying to picture myself in *Breakfast at Tiffany's*, but it doesn't come.

"Sure you do," she says with seriousness in her voice. "You have her long thin neck and her dark hair and dark eyes. All you need is a little makeup and the right clothes."

I'm starting to believe her. If the piles of *Photoplay* she has stacked around her room mean anything, Eva Singer is an expert on movie stars.

"Well," I say, "did anyone ever tell *you* that you look just like Natalie Wood?"

"Oh sure," she says, emery boarding a long polished fingernail—real, not the stick-on kind. "I hear that all the time. Let's go downstairs. I have to practice before my parents get home."

"Yeah. I have to go home anyway," I say, not meaning it. "I have stuff I have to do too."

When I'm halfway out the front door, she calls to me from the piano stool. "Why don't you stop by after school on Monday. We can do homework together."

"Oh, okay. That sounds good," I say as calmly as I can. Inside, my heart is racing to beat the band. Only two more days until I see Eva Singer again. Way to go, God! Keep those bonuses coming.

CHAPTER ELEVEN

——◆——

IT'S AMAZING HOW FAST your luck can turn on you—a chameleon changing its color to match its surroundings. When I get home, I reach for the doorknob and it falls off and drops onto my foot, pounding my big toe like a hammer. I pick it up and try putting it back, but the minute I take my hand away, it falls again and hits the same toe. The door opens, and for a second, I think it might be Allen Funt telling me to SMILE! I'm on *Candid Camera*. Instead of Allen Funt, my grandmother is standing there with her face twisted into a knot.

"What are you trying to do, wreck the place?" The words shoot out of her mouth—poison darts.

The part of me that's Manny wakes up in my head. *That's right, you miserable old hag. I'm going to tear down the whole goddamn house with my bare hands starting with this son of a bitch of a doorknob.* "I was trying to open the door and the knob fell off," I say, holding it out to her as if I have just run over her cat and I'm standing there with the dead body begging her forgiveness. "I didn't mean to do it."

"You didn't mean to end up on my doorstep either, did you?" She spits the words at me and grabs the doorknob out of my hand. "Eating my food and sleeping under my roof. I can't turn

59

around in my own house without having you under my feet. You with your no good father written all over your face."

I stand there looking at *her* face not knowing what to say. She hasn't asked me a question so there's no answer to give. She knows what she's doing when it comes to destroying people. Slapping me across the face would have been kinder than telling me I look like Manny. Besides, I know that I look like my mother when she was my age—my grandpa told me so. Plus, Manny doesn't look one bit like Audrey Hepburn, or even her brother, if she has one.

"Well, are you coming in or not?" She stands back at a safe distance so I won't contaminate her as I walk by. I half expect her to make me hang the doorknob on a chain and wear it around my neck so that everyone will know what a terrible thing I have done—the Hester Prynne of Ridgewood.

"Is there anything you want me to do? The dishes or the wash or anything?" I know the answer because I've heard it so many times before, but I ask anyway.

"What I want you to do is stay out of my way and leave me alone." She slams the front door and heads toward the kitchen, holding the doorknob out far in front of her. A live thing that might turn on her and bite.

I walk toward the stairs to the attic. Behind the attic door are my cot and the bedding Mama and I use. We make sure that we're up and the living room is back in order before my grandmother comes down in the morning. It's not hard to do because she sleeps late. She goes to bed early, and most days, she takes a nap in the afternoon. A day in this house is a combination of pain and pleasure, like going to the dentist. You white-knuckle the arms of the chair and put up with the drilling, but then you can have something from the treasure chest or a free toothbrush. If Grandpa and Mama and I hold on tight and let my grandmother spoil part of our day, we can have the rest of it for ourselves.

The attic is where Mama and I go to hide from my grandmother. She's afraid of spiders and other crawly things so she doesn't come up, and Grandpa has no interest in anything here so we've taken it over. A private place for just the two of us. It's like being back in Phoenix, alone in our suite. We're a strange pair, not a mother and her daughter, not friends who share secrets. We're orphans alone in the world holding onto each other so we don't fall off the edge. Mama didn't learn how to be a mother, and because of that, I don't know how to be a daughter. I don't feel cheated though, so I guess it's true. You don't miss what you've never had.

When we're here together, I sit on the floor with my back against the brick chimney and read a novel I borrowed from the library, and Mama sits in the rocking chair near the little round window and reads her letters. Every time I ask her who wrote them, she makes up a different story. Sometimes they're from her grandfather and sometimes from people she went to school with. Sometimes those letters take her so far away that she doesn't hear me when I talk to her.

I walk over to the little round window I've looked through a hundred times before. Our house is at the top of a hill, so I can see as far as my school. Until now, I never even noticed the red roof of Eva Singer's house. Today it's the only thing I see. It stands out, a red flag, a magnet that keeps pulling my eyes back to it even when I try to yank them away. She's under that roof right now playing the piano, the girl who has awakened an excitement in me that's been asleep just under the surface. An excitement so strong and wild that I didn't know such a thing was possible.

To keep myself from thinking about the shame that is rising in me, I stand on a chair and pull Mama's box of letters down from the high shelf where she hides them when I pretend I'm not looking. I know they aren't for me to see, but they pull me like the red roof does. What is in those letters that has such a power over her that she dreams her way back to Phoenix and Manny every time she reads them? I think they're her red roof, and they take her to a happier time.

I'm holding it. An old-fashioned candy box. Mama has it secured with a blue ribbon that's been tied and untied so many times, it's soiled and frayed, a loyal friend guarding the secrets of her past. This box is the only thing of Mama's that didn't fall prey to my grandmother's revenge. Everything else got thrown away when she left. The punishment for her terrible crime. I untie the ribbon and open the lid. Its scent draws me to it. The memory of chocolate is still there—stale and musty now—but I'm sure that one time long ago, the chocolate was fresh and Mama, as pretty as an Adirondack autumn, was thanking Manny for the gift.

Grandpa must have turned on the furnace, because the chimney is warm on my back when I settle down next to it. The bulb hanging from the ceiling gives off just enough light. It's cozy here, so I don't understand the chill that runs through me when I start reading the letters.

CHAPTER TWELVE

—◆—

SOMETIMES YOU HAVE TO step away from a situation and wonder about it. This is the second day our home ec. class has been learning how to make egg salad sandwiches and we're just now getting to the food part. You'd think we were constructing an atom bomb or at least collecting top secret information for the FBI the way the teacher is all serious about everything. One wrong move and we could destroy the world.

This is not just an ordinary teacher. This is the head of the home economics department of the Ridgewood Teachers' College. She's wearing a white coat like a doctor or one of those scientists you see in the movies holding a test tube full of steaming liquid. Someone doing important work.

We're in the home economics laboratory of the college part of our school. Maybe that's the reason for the white coat. They probably call it a laboratory instead of a kitchen because it sounds more like college. A big deal. Plus, there are six complete kitchens in one big room. All of them have giant mirrors above the prep counters so we won't miss anything important the teacher might do like opening the mayonnaise jar or taking the bread out of the wrapper.

They combine the seventh and eighth grade girls for home ec. while the boys have shop. That right there makes me want

63

to complain to the principal. It would be a lot more fun to wear safety goggles and make a birdhouse than to sit here waiting for the show to start. The only good part of this arrangement is that Eva Singer is two rows ahead of me and I can look at the back of her head any time I want.

You can tell this is a big event because there's a row of college girls in the back of the room taking notes like crazy, so they won't forget anything when they're teachers and ruin a kid's life by teaching egg salad sandwiches wrong. Plus, they're probably going to have to take a test.

So far, we've had a tour of the laboratory and an official lesson on hand washing. You can't just do it the regular way; you have to do it the home ec. way. You roll up your sleeves and take off your rings, if you have any. The water has to be a certain temperature—hot enough to hurt. Once the soap is on, you start lathering in a circular motion, wrists included, and count one Mississippi, two Mississippi until you get to fifteen. If you stop before fifteen, you might just as well forget the whole thing. The germs will still be kicking and you will contaminate everything you touch.

The teacher looks like Mrs. Eisenhower in a hairnet, which covers everything but her bangs. She keeps a fake smile on her face while she's talking to the girls with long fingernails about how they're walking germ factories and they should think seriously about cutting them short. Eva is one of the guilty ones and she gives me a giant eye roll to let me know what she thinks about the whole thing. I bite my nails, so there's no place for germs to hide, unless I forget and bite after I have scrubbed.

Next comes the outline on the chalkboard of the steps we will take to make an egg salad sandwich, only the teacher calls it a flow chart to show how smart she is. Number one is TEST TO SEE IF EGGS ARE FRESH. Every letter is perfect—starched and ironed.

Mrs. Eisenhower looks around to see if all eyes in the room are on the egg she is holding—a jewel so rare and valuable that she can hardly trust herself with it. "*Ladies*," she says with importance in her voice. "You will do well to follow the advice I am about to give you. It will serve you for the rest of your lives."

You can almost *hear* the ears in the room perk up to take in whatever pearls of wisdom this brilliant teacher of future teachers is about to present to us.

"Always use double A eggs. They are the highest grade available. They may cost a little more, but their superior quality and longer shelf life are worth the extra money. Is there anyone who would like me to repeat what I have just said. Anybody?"

The sun was shining for just a second and then a cloudy patch. Is this woman for real? I picture her husband—a cardboard cutout of Father in the Dick and Jane reading books from first grade, all covered with plastic to keep him clean.

"All right, ladies. Stop the talking." She taps a spoon against the counter, scans the room heaving a noticeable sigh, and looks toward the ceiling for guidance. "I must have your attention." She glares at two eighth graders and asks their permission to go on with the lesson. "Thank you," she says when the room is silent. We can see that she is holding a dish of water in one hand and an egg in the other. "You must always test your eggs before you use them. Remember, the only way to attain a perfect end product is to start with perfect ingredients. The way to test the freshness of an egg is by . . . "

I think how this woman would pass out dead if I told her about the food that is served in my house. It sits in my grandfather's store until it's too iffy to sell to his customers and then he brings it home for us.

"Now watch what happens when I put the fresh egg into the bowl of water."

Sometimes you're locked into a predicament that makes you crazy. Somebody's idea of a sick joke. I feel my eye start to twitch and the toe of my shoe is tapping the chair in front of me so hard that the kid who is sitting on it turns and gives me a dirty look. I can see Mrs. Eisenhower's mouth moving, but the words come out all slow motion and garbled.

I picture myself standing up in front of all these people, pummeling her with swearwords for treating us like imbeciles. Two men in white coats come and take me away while everyone watches with fear on her face. When this feeling comes, I have to hold onto my chair and talk myself through it, like in church when the preacher won't shut up. Sometimes I count to a hundred and hope that when I'm finished, the torture will be over.

Today, I look at the clock and see that there's too much time left for counting, so I take myself back to the day in the attic when I read Mama's letters—the day I discovered that Manny isn't my father after all. Mr. Brand, my gym teacher who thinks I'm so great because I can hit a baseball better than any boy in my class, is my father, and the copying fool is my sister.

* * *

Mama has read the letters so many times that the paper is soft like flannel pajamas. The folds have split, and the one in which he tells her he loves her is in pieces and has to be put together like a jigsaw puzzle. This tender Manny surprises me. The words in these letters don't match the man I knew—the one with ice where his heart should be. I look at Mama in a different light. She didn't settle for just anybody. The man she fell in love with wrote such sweet words that I can understand why she thought he would love her forever.

The letter that changes who I am is crisp and clean. The words on the envelope are written in Mama's Palmer writing that she is so proud of, the writing that took thousands of circles to perfect. Under the words *Tommy Brand* she has drawn a curlicue line with two dots above it, the kind of frou-frou she loves.

When I open the envelope, a photograph falls onto my lap like the prize in a Cracker Jack box. I tilt it toward the light, and when I look at it, pretty people in prom clothes stare back at me. I recognize Mr. Brand because he looks the same, like Tony Perkins, only cuter. But Mama takes my breath away.

LETTERS IN THE ATTIC

There she is—Elizabeth Taylor, only prettier. She has told me since I can remember that people used to say she looked like Elizabeth Taylor, but I didn't believe her.

The picture is black and white, but in my mind her dress is pale blue to match her eyes. Her arms are down in front of her gracefully, one hand clasping the other, careful not to muss the corsage pinned to her tiny waist. She is looking at the camera, but her head is bent down shy. Mr. Brand is staring at her as if he has discovered a priceless jewel and refuses to take his eyes away for fear somebody else might take it. They're standing in my grandmother's living room in front of Mama's piano, polished shiny.

This must have been a happy time in this house. I picture my grandmother fussing over that nice Tommy Brand, asking him to sit down and telling him that Veronica will be ready in a minute. Would he like something to drink?

I wonder who took the picture. My grandmother prob-ably. She would never trust Grandpa to do such an important thing.

I remember the Mama of a few hours ago—the one in the waitress uniform and the nurse's shoes, and it scares me to think what life can do to a person.

I put the photograph carefully on my lap with the envelope and I open the letter. While I'm reading it, my heart is beating in my throat and I feel as if I might suffocate because the only breaths I can take come in little gasps. I'm the baby Mama is telling Tommy Brand about, the one she will have in seven months. The one that was made the night of the prom after the picture was taken. His baby, the one he doesn't know about because she never gave him the letter.

I finish reading and then my body relaxes and I can breathe again. The thought of Mr. Brand's being my father brings a warm feeling to my heart. Cross off Manny. He's not a part of me anymore. A ray of sunshine has entered my life that surprises me. You just don't see something like that coming.

* * *

"We don't have time for this nonsense, young lady!" The yelling is an alarm clock waking me from my daydream and I think for a moment that I might be the young lady. I committed the sin of escaping the boredom and I have been found out. "I asked you to read this for the class and you're sitting there as if I'm speaking to you in a foreign language. Now please . . . read this for the class. We're waiting." The teacher is tapping number four on the chalkboard with a wooden pointer: BE SURE BREAD IS COMPLETELY BUTTERED TO PREVENT LEAKAGE OF FILLING.

"I don't know what it says. I can't read it." Eva's words come out in a whisper.

Mrs. Eisenhower fixes her eyes on her, mean—a dog to be kicked for not knowing the command. "What do you mean you can't read it? You're in the eighth grade for heaven's sake. Stop fooling around. We don't have all day." More tapping and waiting. Silence.

Eva's head is down and has all but disappeared into her body. A turtle turning itself into a rock. *This isn't happening*, I think. *It can't be.*

"All right then. Never mind," the teacher says coldly, unlocking her eyes from Eva's face. "You there. You in the white sweater. Will you please read this for the class so we can go on."

I'm the one in the white sweater. The one she has chosen to put Eva Singer in her place. I nearly commit the betrayal before I take time to think about it, and then I say, "I can't read it either."

She looks at me, sighs, and then pulls air into her mouth through clenched teeth. "Well, I can see that some people in the class think this lesson is all fun and games. You two girls can go back to your classrooms and think about what has just happened here. I'll be talking to your teachers about your behavior and I'm sure you'll pay the consequences." Her words are sandpapery, like you'd hurt yourself if you touched them.

I glance back at the row of college girls as we head toward the door. Some of them are watching us. A sideshow at the carnival. The others, the ones who will be getting As, are writing in their notebooks as fast as they can so that when they are teachers, they'll remember what to do with juvenile delinquents.

"Bitch!" Eva says as soon as the door has closed. Her face is molded into hatred. This surprises me. I expected her to be all teary-eyed and mopey like I would have been.

"Yeah," I add, flipping through my brain for Manny's vocabulary. "Goddamn son of a bitch shithead."

"Beth!" she says, throwing her arm around my shoulder. "I've never heard you swear before. You're really good at it." She looks at me and laughs. Her face takes on a different shape and changes back to beautiful.

"Thanks," I say, thinking how everything about her is so perfect.

"I'll meet you by the college pond after school," she tells me as she turns the knob on her classroom door. "We can go to my house and listen to records. I have the new Kingston Trio album."

"Okay," I say, thinking how much I love this girl and how I wish her arm could have stayed around me forever.

"Beth?"

"What?"

"Thanks for what you did back there."

"That's okay. I'll see you later."

CHAPTER THIRTEEN

＊───◆───＊

IT'S SATURDAY MORNING AND I'm walking to my father's house. I'm so nervous; a whole slew of butterflies has taken up residence in my stomach. A family reunion. He lives across town, so I have a lot of time before I get there and plenty of opportunity to chicken out. To keep myself from hightailing it to the safety of the attic, I take my mind back to the day I told Eva about Mr. Brand.

＊   ＊   ＊

Her mother answers the door and makes a big fuss over me. She's one of those people who knows how to act around kids, like she's still one herself. A wind-up toy let loose. This I like in one way, but in another, I never know how to act back.

"Well, if it isn't Miss Beth," she says, giving each word a tap as it comes out of her mouth, like the bouncing ball at the movies.

She's a big woman, sloppy with serious short hair and half glasses on a chain around her neck. I've never seen her in anything but jeans and a man's shirt worn outside loose, no jewelry. There are whispers around school that she's one of *those* women, but how? She's married to a handsome doctor. She has a daughter for heaven's sake—a beautiful girly daughter.

"Hi, Mrs. Singer. Is Eva home?" I say, hoping she has something on the stove and has to get right back to it. My mind is full of myself today. I have finally found the courage to tell Eva my news and I want to do it before I lose my nerve.

"She sure is. Come on in." She holds the door open and tweaks the back of my neck playfully. I'm welcome in this house.

"Eva's in her room," she says, dropping her voice a notch. "I think she's doing homework. Maybe you can help her with it. You're good in school. She gets mad when I try, and her father doesn't have the patience." Sadness creeps over her face that I haven't seen before, disappointment maybe. "Go on up. She'll be glad to see you."

She is not glad to see me. She's in an ugly mood. I can tell by the pimple on her chin and the bottle of Midol on her night stand that I'd better watch my step. I haven't turned into a woman yet, and if this Eva is any indication of what it's going to be like, I would just as soon not.

After I tell her that Mr. Brand is my father, she glares at me and purses her lips strict. "Oh, sure, Beth, in your dreams maybe," she says annoyed like I'm wasting her time. She's sitting on her bed, painting her toenails. Her chin is resting on her knee. Chunks of cotton separate her toes.

"No, really," I say, holding out the letter. "I'm not kidding. I have the proof right here." This gets her attention. She hands me the polish, tells me to do my nails—they need it bad—and takes the envelope from my hand. The photograph falls out and lands on the bedspread.

"Is this your mother?" She says the words like they're polluted.

"Yeah. That's her. And Mr. Brand."

"Well, I can tell that's Mr. Brand, but your mother looks like Jean Simmons."

This isn't what I expected, but it's fine. As far as I'm concerned, Jean Simmons and Elizabeth Taylor are a tossup.

She opens the letter, and I move close to her so I can help with the words. She expects it. When it comes to her reading, we're a team. I'm the guide dog. I smell Youth Dew, her trademark scent, just a hint. She sprays the air and walks through it.

After we've finished, she looks at me hard. Her eyes have turned into binoculars, sweeping over my face, searching for something. Then she says, "Holy shit, you lucky dog. You *weren't* kidding! I don't know why I didn't see it before. You look just like him."

"I told you."

"Well, you know what you have to do *now*, don't you?"

"I have no idea."

"You have to claim him. He's yours."

"How do I do that?"

"First of all, you have to cozy up to your sister."

* * *

As I turn onto Oakwood Avenue, I feel guilty about how I baited Madeline Brand into inviting me to her house. It would have been much easier if I could have said straight out, *May I come to your house, have lunch, steal your father?* When I told her how pretty her ringlets were and that I wished my mother would do that to *my* hair, she wiggled around on the edge of her seat and showed me how her mother combed each curl around her finger until it looked like Shirley Temple's. When I asked if I could hold her doll, she got so excited I thought she was going to wet her pants.

I didn't care that the popular girls were looking at me as if I'd gone mad, because they were a lost cause anyway. Their cliques were closed to the public, and when I got Eva I didn't need them anymore, so I stopped trying.

* * *

I'm standing in front of my father's house, trying it on for size. It fits. It's beautiful—brick with cream trim, black roof and shutters. Before I have time to bask in the moment, the front door flies open and Madeline rushes toward me, asking what took me so long, she's been watching out the window for an hour. A voice inside my head tells me to get out of here while I still can. This is a mistake.

"I thought you changed your mind," she says with such bald-faced eagerness that I'm embarrassed for her. She's wearing the wrong color jeans; brand new with the cuffs rolled up wide stiff, white socks, patent leather flats, and a white ruffly blouse. Eva would call her hopeless, a fashion disaster.

"No, I didn't change your mind," I say, trying to sound as if I want to be here. "I just took my time. It's such a nice day." The thought of spending it with her instead of Eva wraps a blanket of selfishness around my heart that makes me feel ashamed.

She grabs my arm. "Come on, Grammy Brand is here. She's my rich grandmother from Florida. She bought us this house. She's going to help us make cookies."

Maybe this won't be so bad after all. I have a Grammy Brand who makes cookies. "What kind?" I ask while she's yanking on my wrist and pulling me up the sidewalk toward the front door.

"Toll House, *dummy*, what else?"

Well, now. The worm has turned. I don't know about this. Maybe it's her way of telling me that we're on her property and she's the boss, so I'll go along with it. I'm willing to put up with some shit from her to discover the underpinnings of my life.

I am finding that since I'm around Eva so much, I have taken up swearing as a hobby. Mostly in my head, but sometimes it slips out. I'll have to keep a tight hold on myself. I have a feeling that Madeline's mother would have a fit if she knew her baby daughter's new friend has a dirty mouth.

"You must be Elizabeth," the mother says, inspecting me so thoroughly I feel as if I should stand at attention. Her face tells me that she does not approve of the way I'm dressed: worn jeans, sweatshirt, sneakers. It's Saturday for crying out loud. While she's wearing her eyes out staring at my long straight hair, she gives one of Madeline's ringlets a tug and lets it go as if to say, *Eat your heart out.*

Mrs. Brand has skin the color of skim milk—so thin you can see blue veins running around under it like streets on a map. The bright red lipstick she's wearing draws attention to the fact that her mouth is simply a line on her face. Her shoulder-length hair, the color of a cardboard box, is held back by a plastic headband—pink—one I have seen Madeline wear to school. Her eyes are barely blue, easy to ignore unless you're taking inventory like I am. She's short with one of those round shapes where huge breasts sit on her belly, making her look like a robin. When Madeline gets a boyfriend, he'd better take a good look at her mother, because this is what he's going to end up with. This woman couldn't hold a candle to my mother. I nearly wrung myself dry wondering what my father's wife would look like. I could have saved myself some worrying in that department.

"Well, girls," she says in a syrupy voice, "I have some knitting to finish. Why don't you go into the kitchen and help Mother Brand with the cookies. We'll have lunch in about an hour. Tuna broccoli casserole. Madeline's favorite. And, Elizabeth, before you step onto the carpet, you can leave your shoes on the mat by the door. There are some slippettes in that basket. You can wear those while you're here."

Slippettes. What the hell are those?

"Oh, sure, Mrs. Brand. I'll do that right now." Just being around these people makes me want to curse my brains out, and the thought of what we're having for lunch gives me the willies. No wonder Madeline is such a jerk. If my father was taking revenge on my mother for marrying Manny, the joke's on him. It's going to be a snap to get them back together.

"Aren't you going to take off *your* shoes?" I ask Madeline while I'm sitting on the flagstone floor putting on the slippettes, which are hideous crocheted peds. One size fits all, chartreuse.

The basket is full of them, all the same. Woolworth's must have had an ugly-color yarn sale.

"My shoes are new," she says, staring at the hole in my sock. "Besides, this is *my* house, so I can do what I want."

"Oh, okay." I hate this girl so much. I stand up, look down at my feet, and cringe. They've managed to turn me into one of *them*.

"I have to go to the little girls' room," Madeline says, doing a jiggle dance to prove her point. "The kitchen's over there. I'll be right back."

When I walk in, Grammy Brand takes one look at me, clutches her chest, makes a strange little sound in her throat, and has to sit down. At first, I think just the sight of me has given her a heart attack. Then she reaches out her hand, pulls me over to her, and motions for me to sit down on the chair next to her's. She's a pretty woman, not old. She has a classy look that makes me think she should be Eva's grandmother instead of mine: frosted hair, suntanned skin, gold jewelry, diamonds. Her eyes are sad, empty while she looks at my face, like she's searching for a memory she has tucked away in a dim cupboard of her mind. "What's your name, dear?" she asks gently, like a feather settling on the grass.

"Elizabeth McMann," I answer, looking into her dark brown eyes, the same color as mine, even the same green specks. There's a warmth about this grandmother that makes me want to fold myself into her and stay forever.

For a moment she goes somewhere with her memories, and then she asks, "Was your mother's name Veronica Warner?" She says the words in a way that tells me she knows the answer before I give it. "My son used to know her," she says, brushing the hair away from my eyes and anchoring it behind my ears. "They went to school together." She runs her hand down my cheek softly before she stands up, walks to the black marble counter, and takes a wallet out of her purse. "You look just like my daughter," she says, her eyes filling with tears as she hands me the wallet and points to a photograph. "There she is. A drunk driver killed her not long after this picture was taken. She was crossing the street. About your age. Just trying to cross the street." The words wash over me like huge waves of sorrow coming from the depths of her heart.

I look at the photograph and see myself staring back. I don't know what to say, so I keep looking at the picture of my dead aunt until my grandmother takes it from me and returns it to her purse. When the moment has passed and the memory is locked safely away, she comes back to the table, dries her tears with the hem of her apron, and forces a smile onto her face. "Well," she says, "I hope you like to make cookies, Elizabeth."

As she comes into the kitchen, Madeline is still buttoning her jeans, which tells me her hands haven't been anywhere near soap and water. "*I'm* going to do everything. This is *my* job. She can watch," she says, positioning herself at the island in the middle of the kitchen that is so beautiful it could be in a magazine. The ingredients for the cookies are pre-measured in little glass bowls ready to go.

"Maddy, Elizabeth is your guest," Grammy Brand says in a pleasant voice.

"Don't *call* me that! You know my mother doesn't like you to call me that stupid name."

Right here, I would like to grab the wooden spoon out of her hand and clobber her with it. She has this sweet grandmother, bought and paid for with her parents' marriage license, and she treats her like last week's leftovers.

"I don't mind," I say, meaning it. Cooking is near the bottom on my list of favorite things to do. "I'll be happy to watch."

Grammy Brand gives me a look that tells me I've just won a million Brownie points in her book. "All right then, Madeline," she says, "the first thing you do is wash your hands."

"I already did. What do I do now?"

After she has creamed the butter and brown sugar, she decides that making cookies is too much work, so she takes me upstairs

to see her room. As we're leaving the kitchen, I look back at
Grammy Brand. Her hands are on her hips. She puffs out her
cheeks and then lets the air escape—an inner tube deflating.
I give her a look to tell her that I feel the same way, but what
can I do with this spoiled brat who is yanking my arm out of
its socket?

As expensive as this house is, Mrs. Brand has managed to
cheapen it with five and ten cent taste. "This is a very pretty
carpet," I lie, following Madeline up the stairs.

"Thanks," she says, bending down and running her hand
along the avocado shag. "I helped my mother pick out everything."

Uh huh. Why doesn't this surprise me? "Wow! That must
have been quite a job."

"Yeah, it was. Grammy Brand designed the kitchen and she
wanted to hire an interior decorator to do the rest. My mother
convinced her to give *us* the money she would have given the
decorator, and we did it ourselves. She thinks it's important to
put your own personality into your home."

"Good idea." They certainly outdid themselves in that department. After they paid Kresge's, I wonder what they did with the
rest of the money. Probably took a trip to the Riviera.

Before we get to Madeline's room, we pass a bedroom with
twin beds.

"Whose room is *this*?" I ask.

"That's my parents' room. Mine's right down here. Come
on."

I picture a slot machine—cherries straight across! I can feel a
divorce seeping right through the walls of this house. "Where's
your father?" I ask, trying to sound nonchalant.

"He's at an away gymnastics meet. Albany, I think. He'll be
back tomorrow."

She sits down hard on her bed and starts bouncing up and
down as if she's on a trampoline. She's already grown whop-
ping breasts like her mother's and they're flapping themselves

silly. I can see the outline of her bra through her blouse. It's the wide-strap kind—what Eva would call industrial strength. I'm still board-flat, but when I do get some, I want them to be regular like Eva's.

I can't believe that her whole room is decorated in Barbie, even her bedspread and curtains. The stuff isn't even old like she just hasn't gotten rid of it yet. Everything is stiff new. This girl is pathetic.

"I thought Miss Miller was the gymnastics coach," I say, wondering about what she has just told me.

"She is, but she's a queer and my father doesn't think she should be alone with a bunch of eighth grade girls, so he volunteered to be her assistant. To keep an eye on her."

"Oh."

"You *do* know what a queer is, don't you?" she asks like she has the key to a secret treasure chest.

Her words catch me off guard. Is this a test? Have I been wearing my feelings for Eva like a new outfit for everyone to see? My brain comes screeching to a halt and I don't know what to say.

Madeline is standing next to me with her hands on her hips. "You *don't* know what it is, do you?" she says with satisfaction in her voice. "I thought you knew everything."

Okay, this is safe. She doesn't have a clue. "No, I don't. What is it?"

"It's a woman who likes to kiss other women. I can't believe you didn't know that!"

"Well, I do now. Thanks."

"You're welcome. My father thinks that they shouldn't be allowed to be teachers. The only reason they want to be near kids is so they can mess around with them and make *them* queer too."

"Oh!" Her words make me feel as if I've been thrown into a tub of ice water. I walk over to her vanity and stare into the mirror, but I don't see myself at all, just a stranger looking back—ashamed.

"What's the matter with you?" she asks. "You look like you've seen a ghost. Is all this talk about queers making you sick? That's what my father says. They make him sick."

Anger slams into me hard—a punch in the stomach. "I have to go home now, Madeline." I head toward her bedroom door and she follows me close.

"You can't go yet," she whines. "You didn't look at my doll collection. We haven't had lunch. We still have to play Sorry. You said you were going to spend the whole day." Her words tumble over each other like a litter of puppies in a box.

By the time I get my sneakers on, Mrs. Brand is standing next to me. "What do you think you're doing?" she asks in a teacher's voice. "Where are your manners? The table is set for four."

When I get to the end of the sidewalk, I stop and look back at my father's house. Madeline and her mother are on the front step with their arms folded in front of them. Then my eye catches movement in one of the windows. My grandmother is watching me. Just before I turn to go, she raises her hand to her mouth and sends me a kiss, small, but it was there. I saw it.

I need to get away from this place. I start racing down the street as if my feet have wings. I think if I run fast enough, my thoughts won't be able to catch up with me and I'll stop feeling like I want to die.

*   *   *

The attic is dark. I don't bother to turn on the light. I'm not in the mood to read or do anything at all. There's an overwhelming misery in my heart, and I wonder why growing up has to be such a hard thing to do. My insides feel as if someone is squeezing me around the middle so that I can't take a full breath. My thoughts are shuffling around in my head like a pack of cards gone flying. My father thinks I'm a freak, so it must be true. I'm someone to stay away from, to make fun of—a leper.

Out of nowhere, a thought enters my head that sweeps the blackness out of my mood. Nobody knows about me, and I'll never tell. That will be easy enough. It isn't as if the word queer is written on my face. I'll tuck all of this into a secret corner of my mind and leave it there, buried forever. Besides, I'm probably wrong about the whole thing. My imagination has been playing tricks on me. That's all this is. I'll prove it to myself. I'll change into a girly girl and I'll get a boyfriend. Plus, I'll never hit another baseball as long as I live. I'll turn myself into a helpless little priss. That will take care of it. My stomach relaxes and I can breathe again.

I turn on the light and get Mama's letters from the shelf. I take the Tommy Brand envelope out and return the box to its hiding place. The Adirondack autumn has stripped the trees naked, so Eva's red roof stands out stark against the gray October sky. The round attic window has rusted on its hinges. It makes a squealing sound when I push it open. The pieces of the letter are so tiny that when I hand them over to the wind they look like early flakes of snow. I tear the photograph perfectly so that only Mama is left. I put her in my pocket, careful not to bend her. Then I add the other half of the picture to the snowstorm. Cross off Mr. Brand.

CHAPTER FOURTEEN

THE SCHOOL NURSE IS putting a thermometer in a little girl's mouth when I get to her office. She tells me to sit down on the chair next to the sink; she'll be right with me. I cannot believe what is happening. It just goes to show that you can be walking along through your life with all the pieces in place, then POW! You crash into a plate glass window you didn't even know was there, and the whole world is pointing and laughing like you're the bearded lady in the circus.

"Now, what can I do for *you*?" the nurse asks, taking a note from my hand. When she opens it, I see my name and the words *Menstrual Accident* written with the red pen Mr. Stephens was using to correct papers when I went to his desk to ask for help with a math problem. Just before Madeline yelled, "Hey, look! She's got the curse all over the back of her skirt."

Before Mr. Stephens wrote the note, he took off his sweater. As he was tying it around my waist, he said as kind as anything, "Wait and see, Elizabeth. Everything will be all right." Everything is *not* all right. The worst possible thing that could happen to anybody has landed on me.

83

"Is this your first period?" the nurse asks, leaning toward me close, talking softly.

I nod. Then, as if her words have pushed the sad button on my heart, tears I didn't know were coming spill onto my cheeks and huge sobs grab hold of my body and shake the daylights out of it. The thermometer girl's eyes widen and her face takes on a concerned look while she watches as the nurse hands the big crybaby a Kleenex.

I think how a few minutes ago I was a kid, and now I'm a woman who can get pregnant. I don't think God should spring important things like that on you whenever He feels like it. You should have time to get used to the idea, and then when you're ready you say, Okay. Now!

The nurse opens a cabinet, brings out a flat pink box, and hands it to me. "Here you are, Elizabeth. This is everything you'll need." Then she starts rummaging around in a plastic laundry basket on the other side of the sink. "Okey-dokey," she says. "I think these will fit." She gives me some jeans and a pair of underpants, not new. "Don't worry," she says when she sees the look on my face. "They're clean. I took them home and put them through my own washer and dryer. We have these kinds of emergencies all the time."

She is not fooling me. I know the kinds of emergencies she's talking about are kindergartners wetting their pants and throwing up on themselves.

"Go ahead into the bathroom and change now," she says. "Do you know how the belt works?"

"Oh, sure," I lie, wishing I were home. But then, only my grandmother would be there, so I take back the wish and head toward the bathroom. Just before I close the door, I glance over at the little girl. She gives me a hint of a smile, and I think that if I had a baby sister, she's the one I would want.

"Was your mother Veronica Warner?" the nurse asks when I come out of the bathroom, holding the soiled clothes that I've rolled into a ball to hide the evidence of the crime scene. She's sitting at her desk, looking at a folder.

"Yes," I answer, wondering how I'm going to get out of returning to my classroom. The jeans I'm wearing are so tight that anybody who looks my way is sure to see the outline of the Kotex that is so huge, it feels as if there's a blanket stuffed between my legs. Even the *word* Kotex sounds disgusting as it echoes in my head. I hate it. I hate this whole shitty thing. I wish it would all just go away.

The nurse doesn't stare, which makes me think how polite some people can be. Maybe she'll take pity on me and let me go home.

"Your mother and I went to school together," she goes on, nodding toward a brown grocery bag on the counter and gesturing for me to put my dirty clothes in it. "We were best friends. My name is Bertha, but back then, everybody called me Bertie."

I say the first thing that comes into my head. "Where's Martha?"

"So your mother told you about us," she says, patting the chair next to her desk for me to sit down. "We were the Three Musketeers all through high school. Your mom was a real knockout. The boys nearly killed themselves trying to get her attention."

A thought takes her away for just a minute, and then she continues down memory lane. "Martha and I were the plain Janes of the group. The only time we got dates was when Veronica fixed us up. Martha's a nun now, Sister something or other. I lost touch with her when she entered the convent. She promised to write, but she never did."

She scans my face as if she's searching for a clue to a mystery. "So, tell me about your mother. What's she up to? The last I heard she ran away with Manny McMann and was living down south somewhere. Nobody could understand that. She sure fooled everybody. We all thought she was going to marry another boy, but lucky for her, she didn't. She ducked a bullet on that one. Is Manny back in town, too?"

"No. They're divorced. She's working at Major's Drug Store," I say, thinking how things have gotten interesting all of a sudden. "How did she meet Manny again? She told me, but I can't remember."

"Oh, he was the groundskeeper at the golf course. Your grandfather used to take your mother there all the time. She was his little princess. He took her everywhere."

"Did my mother play golf?"

"Oh, goodness no," she says, shaking her head and talking to me as if we're classmates. "She just went along to be with him. She was a real daddy's girl. I think it made your grandmother jealous. Can you imagine being jealous of your own daughter?"

I shake *my* head and think how much trouble Bertie would be in if the principal could hear what she was saying.

"Anyway, she used to tell us how Manny made passes at her when your grandfather wasn't looking and wrote her letters that he would leave in a secret place for her to find. She used to go on about those letters and tell us how charming he was. Martha and I thought she was just going through a phase, but I guess not. I think she was looking for somebody who would take her as far away from your grandmother as possible."

She takes the papers out of my folder, straightens them, and puts them back. "All right, now I've said too much. Once my mouth starts running I can't seem to put on the brakes. Let's just keep what I've told you between us, okay?"

"I won't say anything," I say, thinking how becoming a woman creates an automatic bond with other women that makes them spill their guts. "My mother told me all that stuff. I just forgot."

"Okay, Elizabeth. Who do you want me to call to take you home?" she asks, returning to her nurse's voice. "I'm sure you don't want to go back to class, and walking home in that outfit might get you arrested. I'm sorry about those pants, but they're the only ones I have that are close to your size."

"That's all right. You can call my grandfather. He'll come and get me. What happened to the little girl who was here?"

Bertie glances at the empty chair, sighs, and then shakes her head. "She's one of my regulars. She got over her tummy ache and went back to kindergarten. Her mother died a few months ago. She just needs a little extra attention."

"Oh!" The force of what she has said makes me feel hollow at the center and ashamed of myself for acting like such a baby. You have to wonder about the wrongfulness of something like that.

While I'm waiting for my grandfather, the secretary from the principal's office comes in all fluttery. When she sees me, she motions with her head for Bertie to come over to her. She's so excited she can hardly contain herself. I look out the window and act as if I'm busy with thoughts of my own and that what she's about to say is of no interest to me.

"They got him," she says in a low voice.

"Who?"

"Tom Brand. The police went to the gym and took him away right in the middle of a class."

"You're kidding!"

"No, I'm not. They came and asked me where to find him. I saw the whole thing, handcuffs and everything. I guess enough parents finally came forward."

"It's about time. He's a sick son of a bitch. He *should* be behind bars."

"I've got to get back," the secretary says. "I can hear my phone ringing. Watch the six o'clock news."

"Elizabeth," Bertie says, sitting back down at her desk, "do you feel crampy? Do you want an aspirin?" I can tell by the look on her face that her mind is somewhere else—in jail, I think—and she doesn't really hear me when I say, "No, thanks."

* * *

When we get home, I change into my pajamas and my grandfather tucks me into his bed and tells me that he hopes I feel better. He doesn't ask me any questions about my sickness, which I think is so considerate of him, because I know he knows. When he came to pick me up, Bertie sent me to wait in the car, and when he finally did come out, he joked around about having his ear talked off.

* * *

I didn't realize how tiring becoming a woman is until I feel my mother shaking me awake and telling me that supper is ready.

"I'm sorry you had to go through this in school," she says, stroking my forehead gently with her cool, smooth hand. "I was hoping it would happen at home so I could be there for you."

It feels strange to have her touch me in such an affectionate way, because she isn't usually like this. When I look at her, I see that her eyes have welled up. I think she's remembering when this happened to *her*, and I'm pretty sure that my grandmother is mixed in with those tears.

"It was no big deal," I say, enjoying this soft side of her. "Your friend Bertie is the school nurse. She helped me."

"I know. Daddy told me. She wants me to call her."

* * *

As the news comes on, the whole family is in the living room as usual. Mama, Grandpa, and my grandmother are lined up on the couch as if they're waiting for a bus. I'm sitting on a chair by the window where I can see all of their faces perfectly.

When Mr. Brand's face fills the screen, my grandmother lets out a gasp and drops her knitting into her lap. My mother's back stiffens and she tosses me a glance. She hasn't mentioned the missing letter and the fact that I know about him. I think she's hidden it away in a dark corner of her mind with the rest of the debris from her life. My grandfather doesn't look surprised. I'm sure Bertie has already filled him in.

The newscaster tells us that Mr. Thomas Brand, a native son and a popular physical education teacher at the Ridgewood Campus School, has allegedly been molesting female students for several years. However, until now, there has not been enough evidence to arrest him. The families of eight girls have filed charges and more are pending. Mr. Brand has a wife and a daughter who is the same age as his alleged victims. Because of the serious nature of the allegations and the large number of complaints, the judge has denied bail and Mr. Brand will be remanded to the county jail to await indictment. We should watch the eleven o'clock broadcast for any new details about the case.

The couch people have turned to stone, and when I look at my mother's face with her jaw clenched and her eyes filled with hate, my brain starts working overtime. The pit of my stomach feels as if a vise is crushing it when the thought comes to me that she was one of his victims. Maybe Bertie was wrong. Maybe it wasn't my grandmother that Mama wanted to get away from when she married Manny. Maybe it was that nice Tommy Brand.

*   *   *

All the time I spent worrying about going back to school and being teased because of what happened to me the day before was wasted. I was saved by Madeline's disaster. As I listen to tongues wagging all around me, I look over at her empty desk and feel sorry for her. It isn't her fault she's so weird. Besides, nobody deserves what she must be going through. Word has it that she and her mother have already left to live with relatives in Iowa. I think of Grammy Brand in Florida and wonder if she knows. I picture her on a sunny patio entertaining a friend when the call comes. It makes me sad to think how trouble can find you when you're just sitting there, minding your own business, sipping iced tea.

CHAPTER FIFTEEN

MAMA HAS A BLIND DATE with my teacher. As it turns out, he isn't married and he doesn't have any kids and it's a gigantic mystery to me how somebody that nice has escaped being caught for so long. If we do everything right, maybe *we* can catch him. He is *way* better than I ever dared hope for. He's like wishing for a nickel and getting Fort Knox. I've heard about people's lives having peaks and valleys. Well, Mr. Stephens is more than a peak. He's Mt. Everest.

Bertie arranged the whole thing. As soon as she and Mama found each other, they picked up their friendship right where it left off. Bertie's husband is the head of the maintenance department at the college. He and Mr. Stephens are on the same bowling team, and they sing together in a barbershop quartet. Plus, they live right next door to each other in a small town ten miles north of Ridgewood. They even carpool to work.

Lucky for us I had my menstrual accident in school instead of at home. It's funny how fate takes you by the hand and leads you in the right direction. You might have to walk through some muck to get there, but in the end it's all worth it.

I'm in my grandfather's room helping Mama get ready for a Halloween party at the Knights of Columbus hall. Costumes are optional, so she's not wearing one.

"It's going to be bad enough going out with somebody I've never met without making a complete fool of myself," she says while I'm trying to convince her to be a good sport and wear the fortune teller costume Bertie lent her. "I don't know why I let her talk me into this. I have half a mind to call and cancel."

Well, damn it all to hell. You can just put that half of your mind where the sun doesn't shine and try to think straight with the other half. Luckily, my brain says *Hold it! Stop right there!* before the words slip out, kill my mother, and ruin the whole thing.

"You don't have to wear a costume," I say light and cheery, holding the new dress she bought for the occasion out in front of me. "I bet most of the people there won't have costumes on." I steal a glance in her direction and am relieved to see her putting on the new Revlon Fire and Ice lipstick she bought to match her outfit.

"Tell me again what he looks like," she says, blotting her mouth with a Kleenex.

I've told you a million times. He looks nice. "He's about three or four inches taller than you, brown hair, brown eyes I think, a little on the chubby side, but not fat. Just nice."

"What does he usually wear? Is he well groomed?"

You're asking me that? You used to sleep in the same bed with Manny McMann for crying out loud! "Brown," I say, trying to remember the color of the sweater he tied around my waist. "Yeah, he wears brown mostly. Corduroy pants, button-down shirts, cardigan sweaters, loafers. He's nice and clean and he smells good. Aqua Velva, I think."

"You make him sound like Rock Hudson," she says in a giggly voice. "All except the chubby part."

"He's not really chubby," I say quickly, wishing I'd left that out.

"Oh, I don't care if he's fat. I just don't want him to be disappointed when he sees *me*."

"He's not going to be disappointed. You look beautiful. You look just like Elizabeth Taylor."

"Lizzy! You're really somebody," she says, sitting on the bed and pulling me down next to her. She looks at me deep, as if she can see right through to my soul. "I'm sorry your life's been such a roller coaster ride. I didn't want you to have to grow up like this. I can see how much tonight means to you and I'll try my best. That's all I can do."

I look into her eyes and I think how she lives life straight from her heart. "I love you, Mama."

"I love you too."

* * *

The first thing I notice when I open the door is the two-pound box of Russell Stover chocolates Mr. Stephens is holding, and I think that's just the sweetest thing. He didn't even wait until he tried my mother out to see if she's worth spending the money. That right there tells you what kind of person he is. He's all dressed up—navy blue pinstripe suit, red paisley tie, black polished shoes. His scent matches his clothes. Classy, not Aqua Velva.

"Hi there, Elizabeth. Happy Halloween," he says, reaching into his pocket and handing me my own miniature box of Russell Stovers. Right here, I think I love this man.

"Thanks, Mr. Stephens," I say, hoping Mama will hurry up because I don't know what to say to a teacher when he's standing in my living room, wearing different clothes, being my mother's date.

"Are your grandparents here?" he asks. "I was hoping to meet them." Even though his words sound sincere, I think Bertie must have filled him in about my grandmother and he wants to see for himself if what she said is true.

"No. Well, my grandmother's here, but she's sleeping and my grandfather is down at his store protecting his plate glass windows. Last year it took him a whole week to clean off the soap."

"Ah . . . I see," he says, sounding as if what I've just said seems perfectly normal. "So you're going to man the door here for the trick or treaters."

Before I have to tell him that nobody is going to man the door and that I'm going trick or treating with Eva and then spend the night at her house, Mama comes into the room.

I know that she's going to be impressed, so I watch *his* face. A bit of a smile shows up and there's a look in his eye that tells me we've passed the first test. While he's introducing himself, he waits for her to offer her hand so he can shake it. I read in a book, that is the proper way. The boy should be ready and waiting, but he never makes the first move. If the girl doesn't stick out her hand, he should forget the whole thing. It doesn't surprise me that he's perfect in the manners department too.

Mama makes a big fuss about the candy and doesn't mention the fact that she has joined Weight Watchers and wouldn't touch one of those chocolates if she were stranded in the middle of the ocean on a rubber raft and they were all there was to eat.

After the door has closed behind them, I crouch down, park my chin on the sill, and peer out the front window. As Mr. Stephens opens the car door for my mother, the light goes on and I can see Bertie and her husband in the back seat—Mr. and Mrs. Potato Head. Bertie made their costumes out of papier-mâché, Mama said. As the car backs down the driveway, I say a quick prayer and ask God to let Mr. Stephens fall in love with my mother. Then I grab my coat and head over to Eva's.

* * *

"You owe me for this," Eva says, mean bossy. "You owe me *big* time. If anybody I know sees me like this I'm going to kill you, and then I'm going to kill myself."

"Good! Kill yourself. See if I care," I say, sounding as rotten as I can. I've just about had it with her moods. She has a dark, ugly place in her heart that has been showing itself a lot lately. "I didn't exactly have to twist your arm. You wanted to come just as much as I did."

She mumbles something I can't make out and pulls ahead of me to show that she will not give up her position. You have to get used to that kind of thing when you're the younger half of a friendship.

I have never been trick or treating before. Mama and Manny always had to work parties on Halloween and I had to stay in our room, so I'm genuinely excited about the whole thing. I ease up on Eva in case she decides to pull a pout and head home. "It'll be fun," I say in a chipper voice. "We won't see anybody we know way down here."

We're walking toward the big houses by the lake where the really rich people live. The ones with maids who wear uniforms, *old money* my grandfather calls them. Eva's dressed in her grandmother's wedding gown. I'm the groom in one of Dr. Singer's old suits. My hair is tucked into a fedora and a black cardboard mustache is clipped to my nose. It pinches.

It takes forever for the lady in the first house to answer the bell. We can see her peek around the curtain on the window next to the door and then we hear her fiddling with the lock. I can actually taste the chocolate bar she'll give us—Nestle's Crunch, probably, or Hershey's with almonds. Anyone who lives in a house *this* fancy is sure to give full-size candy bars, not the one-bite kind.

When the woman finally gets the door open, she says, "Well, do tell! I never expected *you* to stop by." Then she invites us in. The house smells like Ben Gay. "Now, tell me who you are again," she says, looking us up and down for a clue. "My memory isn't what it used to be."

After we tell her our names, she asks Eva if her father is Dr. Singer. Then she goes on for ten minutes with the gory details of her gall bladder operation and how he didn't charge a fortune like most doctors these days. She asks Eva to turn around so she can see her veil and then she tells us the entire story of her daughter's wedding and how she never gets to see her grand-children because her son-in-law took a job in California right after the wedding. She's lucky if she gets to see them every ten years. She's sure they would walk right by her on the street and not even recognize her. She thanks us for stopping by and starts to open the door. "You be sure to tell your father that Agnes Bryce sends her best," she tells Eva.

"Trick or treat!" I say before it's too late.

"Goodness gracious!" Agnes Bryce says, smacking her fore-head.

"I don't know where my mind has gone. I didn't buy candy because hardly any children come down this way anymore, but I think I can find something. You wait right here."

I look over at Eva. Her arms are crossed in front of her. Her eyes are locked on mine furious, and nothing comes from her but the sound of breath being blown out her nose.

We wait so long, I think Mrs. Bryce forgot about us and went to bed. Finally, she comes toward us with a box of prunes in her hand.

"I'm sorry I don't have two," she says, dropping it into the pillowcase Eva is holding. "My shopping day is Wednesday, so if you want to come back then, I'll have another one."

"That's okay," Eva says in a snotty tone. "We'll share this one."

Mrs. Bryce must not have heard the edge in Eva's voice, because she tells her in a sweet way to hold up the skirt of her beautiful gown when she's walking down the stairs so she doesn't ruin it like her daughter ruined hers.

On the way to the next house, Eva says, "Here, you probably need these," and she stuffs the prunes into my pillowcase. Then we agree that we aren't going to be suckered into standing around talking to old ladies. If we don't get our rich-people candy with just a *trick or treat*, we'll hear our mothers calling and leave.

The next house we come to looks promising. It's huge and newer looking than the other ones on the street. We figure we'll get some really good loot here.

Dr. Redman, Eva's dentist, answers the door, and I watch as her body deflates. "Well, *Eva*," he says sternly, "I'm surprised to see *you*. Aren't you a little old for this kind of thing?"

"Oh, we're not doing this for *ourselves*," she says quickly with a giggle. "My friend here . . . well, her two little brothers have, um, strep throat and, uh, we told them we'd trick or treat for them." She gives me a look that says, *Shit, Beth. Help me out here.*

"Yeah," I say. "They're really sick. Poor little guys. Twins, three years old. The doctor isn't sure if they'll pull through."

Eva's eyes shoot arrows into mine and then she pinches my leg between her fingernails so hard that I expect to feel blood run down it.

Our really good loot turns out to be apples, and I think I can hear my mother calling me when Dr. Redman starts in on us. "They're nature's candy," he says, placing them into our pillowcases so carefully it's as if he thinks they might break if he drops them. He asks us if we know that his own teenage children have never even tasted candy. We tell him we didn't know that. Then he asks us if we think they miss it. When we don't answer, he says all serious, "Well, they don't. If you think of candy as poison, you'll hate it."

"Right. Good idea," Eva says, backing down the steps two at a time. "Thanks for telling us that and thanks for the apples. They look delicious."

"Yeah, thanks," I say as he's closing the door. "My brothers are going to love them."

Eva turns her hand into a pistol and holds it to her head. "He's such a pain in the ass. Can you believe I have to listen to that shit every six months?" The words spew from her mouth like they're making her sick.

"He *is* pretty creepy," I say, expecting her to tell me that she's finished with this trick or treat crap and she's going home.

When she doesn't, I hide my surprise and follow her down the street.

The next house is dark except for the front porch and some rooms way in the back. "I know who lives here," she says as we get closer. "This is old Judge Spencer's house. He hates Jews and Negroes, even Catholics. Anybody who isn't just like him. He tried to get the medical board to refuse my father hospital privileges when we first moved here. He's a real jerk. Let's see what he's handing out to little Jew girls tonight."

Well, now. This is a side of her that I haven't seen before. Her face means business as she turns onto the brick sidewalk leading up to the house. She walks toward the front door as if she has a purpose, and I have to scramble to keep up with her. As she rings the doorbell, her eyes are ready for battle.

"I don't think anybody's home," I whisper. "Let's get out of here." I'm so nervous I feel like my motor's running.

She ignores me as if I'm an unpleasant memory and rings the bell again. When nobody answers this time, she pulls up the skirt of the wedding dress, reaches into the pocket of her jeans, hands me a toothpick, and tells me to break it in half. When I look at her as if she's lost her mind, she bores her eyes into mine and says, "Just do it!" While I'm doing it, she takes a chunk of soap out of her other pocket and smears the windows on either side of the door. Then she holds down the doorbell, locks it there with the toothpick pieces, and tells me to follow her—fast!

From behind the hedge on the edge of his property, we watch Judge Spencer open the front door, shake his fist at the air, and curse into the night. He yells that we're nothing but a bunch of juvenile delinquents and that it should be against the law for hooligans like us to go begging at respectable people's houses. He hopes we left fingerprints because he's going to throw the goddamn book at us. Then we hear a woman yelling for him to stop ringing the doorbell. This time he aims his profanity at the voice coming from *inside* the house.

We don't wait around to see what happens next. We're definitely too old for this. Besides, rich people have absolutely no idea what Halloween is all about. Eva has taken off her costume and has crammed it into her pillowcase. I have to leave everything on except the hat and mustache, so she takes pity on me and shows me a back way to her house.

Mrs. Singer is dressed in a clown costume complete with happy face makeup. She's handing out popcorn balls to a stoop full of kids. "That didn't take long," she chirps. "Did you have a good time?"

"Oh, yeah," Eva says. "It was a real hoot. I can't wait until next year so I can do it again."

When the doorbell stops ringing, Mrs. Singer comes into the family room where we're watching TV and says, "Well, Eva . . . did you tell Beth your news?"

"No, I forgot," she says, not taking her eyes off the television screen.

"Eva's going to be a big sister," Mrs. Singer tells me with excitement in her voice. "I'm going to have a baby in March. Isn't that great?"

Well, here I have a problem. I'm being pulled in two directions—the rope in a tug of war. Eva doesn't have to say a word to let me know how *she* feels about the whole thing. On the other hand, her mother is about to explode with happiness. "WOW! That's really . . . wow," I say, checking out Eva's face for a reaction. There is none.

"How would you girls like me to make you a pizza and some homemade milkshakes?" Mrs. Singer asks, walking through Eva's mood with blinders on.

I'm about to say how fantastic that would be because I'm starving when Eva says, "Nah . . . we're going to bed. It's late."

"Late?" her mother teases. She sits down next to Eva and pulls her hair playfully. "It's only nine o'clock. It's Saturday night for heaven's sake. Lighten up. Live a little."

"Damn it, Mom! I don't want any crap-ass pizza. Come on, Beth. Let's go to bed." She stands up and heads for the stairs, not looking at anybody.

This is one of those times when it would be nice to be able to crawl in a hole and come out when it's over. Mrs. Singer's painted-on face beams with joy, but her sad eyes give her away. I don't know what to do or what to say, so I look at the floor and follow Eva. I can't figure her out. She's a riddle without any clues.

"What's the matter?" I ask when we're nearly upstairs. "Don't you feel well?"

"I feel fine."

"Well, why did you get so upset with your mother? Aren't you excited about the baby?"

"Oh, *sure* . . . I'm really excited about the fact that my parents have been trying for years to have a baby to make up for the defective one they got stuck with. My mother's had a million miscarriages and they still kept trying to have a normal kid. Well, now they're getting their wish. Goody for them."

"Maybe they just want another child," I say, thinking that's probably the case.

"Beth, I've seen the look in my father's eyes when he has to go to school to pick up my report card and talk to my dumb-class teachers. My parents were college sweethearts for God's sake. I'll be lucky if I make it through high school. They're even talking about sending me away to a private school next year. What can I say? I'm a major disappointment." Her eyes are glazed sad and her look tells me it's hopeless. Her well of happiness has run dry.

*   *   *

Eva's been asleep for hours. I'm lying beside her wide awake, listening to her breathing and thinking how complicated she is. On the outside, she's wrapped in this perfect package, looking like she has all her ducks in a row. On the inside, there's a storm brewing like the one outside her window. I listen to the grumble of thunder and watch as lightning tears bright strips in the black sky.

CHAPTER SIXTEEN

—◆—

THE MAN IN THE BOOTH at the border crossing asks if we're American citizens. He says it first in French, and when nobody answers, he switches to English just like that, which makes me wonder why, if he's so smart, he would choose such a boring job. He could be a translator for the UN or something interesting like that. After asking us the purpose of our trip, how long we'll be staying, and if we'll be leaving anything in Canada, he tells us to have a good time and waves us on.

I'm in the back seat of Mr. Stephens' brand new station wagon. Before he met my mother, he drove a rusted VW Bug. If you ask me, that right there is a gigantic hint about his intentions.

He and my mother and I are on our way to Old Montreal. I pretend that we're a family and we do this sort of thing all the time—get dressed up and go to a foreign country for dinner in a fancy restaurant. Then I tell my brain to cut it out before I jinx the whole thing.

I can see that he's crazy about my mother by the way he looks at her and how he's always complimenting her about every little thing. I also know that Manny is still alive and well in her head and that he's sitting right smack between the two of them ruining everything. Since she and Mr. Stephens have been dating, she reads Manny's letters more than ever, which makes me want to shake her silly and say, Can't you see what's happening here? This is your big chance. Grab it! Life isn't going to wait around while you make up your mind.

"Is this your first time in Canada, Elizabeth?" Mr. Stephens asks as if he really wants to know, like I'm a regular person, not just a kid. He looks back at me in the rearview mirror so I don't feel left out.

"Yes, it is," I say, "and it was so nice of you to invite me." I think if I try extra hard, maybe it will make up for Mama's lack of enthusiasm.

"How about you, Veronica? You've probably been to Montreal dozens of times." He looks over at her with his face full of love, maybe. It dawns on me that I don't know what man-woman love looks like since I haven't had any experience with it. The stuff you see on television doesn't count because it's not real. Plus, nobody could go around their whole life looking cow-eyed like those people.

"This is my first time too," Mama says nice enough, just not as romantic as I want her to be. Maybe I'm wrong about her. Maybe inside she's overflowing with excitement and just doesn't know how to act around somebody who's good to her.

"I hope you both enjoy the restaurant," Mr. Stephens says. "It used to be a stable where the city people kept their horses before cars were invented." I like how he knows things, not like Manny who would be stumped if somebody asked him to name the president.

While they make pleasant conversation, I look out the window at the Canadian countryside—flat with miles of farm fields plowed black, waiting for winter. My mind takes me by the hand and we go back to Mr. Stephens' house.

After he picks us up, we stop there so he can show us around. The first thing I notice is this is a one-person house. Everything is small—living room-kitchen combination, bedroom, bathroom—that's it, except for the screened-in porch off the back door. This is a man's place, plain, no knickknacks. Another thing I notice is there's no TV—just books, lots of books, plus piles of *Field and Stream* magazines.

"Are you a hunter?" I ask, hoping he'll say no.

"No," he says, opening the front door to let in a huge yellow cat. "I don't hunt, but I love to fish . . . trout mostly. There's nothing more relaxing than standing in a stream in a pair of waders, waiting for a strike. Maybe you'd like to come along sometime, Veronica."

Now *that's* something I'd stand in line to see.

"Oh, sure. That sounds like fun," Mama says as if she means it.

I turn my attention to the ball of fur with a tail that's rubbing its head against Mr. Stephens' knees. "Is that your cat?" The words escape before I can catch them. I'm such a moron. Who else would it belong to?

"Yep. This is Captain Queeg."

"From the *Caine Mutiny*?" I ask.

"Yes. It's one of my favorites."

"Mine too. Have you read *Marjorie Morningstar*?"

"If Wouk's written it, I've read it." He goes over to a shelf, pulls out a book, and hands it to me. "Here's his latest, *Youngblood Hawke*. You can borrow it," he says, putting his hand on my shoulder. "You know, Veronica, this kid of yours is really something. She's the one I can always count on when nobody else knows the answer."

Well, now he's done it. I feel like throwing my arms around him and asking him to marry *me*.

Mama gives me a look that says she's proud of me and then she looks at Mr. Stephens and asks, "Did you build this house yourself?"

"No. Bertie and Ralph built it for Bertie's mother. Then she moved to Florida, so I snapped it up. I don't own it, I rent it. It's just right . . . "

"Lizzy, Mr. Stephens asked if you can see the skyline. We're getting close to Montreal." Mama's voice brings me back to Canada, and when I look out the window, the flat land is gone and buildings have taken its place.

Mr. Stephens says, "Heads up," and flips a quarter over the seat and it lands in my lap. "After Paris, Montreal is the largest French-speaking city in the world," he says, scanning the tall buildings just ahead. "It's built around a mountain on an island, so we have to go over a bridge to get there. This one's the Jacques Cartier. It's named for the French explorer who discovered the St. Lawrence River. There's a tollbooth coming up, Elizabeth, so you can fling that coin into the basket. I'd do it myself, but I have terrible aim."

I think it's so cute how he keeps his teacher hat on even when he's not in school. It's like having a private tutor free of charge. Plus, how he knocks himself down to build you up. Usually it's the other way around.

*　*　*

When our waiter brings the menus, Mr. Stephens convinces Mama to go off her diet just for tonight. "The rack of lamb here is out of this world," he says. "Besides, I don't know why you're on a diet anyway. You're perfect just the way you are."

Well, if that doesn't do it, she's completely nuts. She blushes and tells him he's just saying that, while I wonder about the other women he's brought here. I look around the room and I don't see one single man eating alone.

Mama orders lamb, and Mr. Stephens and I take the Dover sole. I'm not crazy about fish, but if he'd ordered pigs' noses, I would have ordered them too.

After the salad course, the waiter puts little dishes of butter in front of us, which turns out to be sorbet. "Well, I guess they want us to cleanse our palates," Mr. Stephens says when he sees Mama and me sitting there like idiots, staring at the foreign food.

"Right," I say, picking up the spoon that looks as if it's part of a kid's tea set. It tastes so good I wish they hadn't been so stingy.

After we finish our chocolate mousse and wash our hands in the finger bowls, I ask Mr. Stephens where the ladies' room is and excuse myself. He tells me to wait a minute and then hands me a dollar. When I give him a puzzled look, he smiles and says, "For the attendant."

I wish Eva could see this bathroom. It's disguised as a fancy living room, as if rich people don't have to pee like the rest of us. The main part has thick rose carpet and long flowered couch-chairs like you see in movie stars' bedrooms in *Photoplay* where they're draped over them in their negligees, smoking cigarettes in long black holders. Each one has a table next to it with magazines—all French—and dishes of mints. If you get tired in the middle of your meal, you come in here, take a nap, read a magazine, and have a mint—just like that.

The bathroom part doesn't have stalls like regular ones do. It has rows of little rooms with actual doors—white with curvy brass handles. A lady in a gray maid's uniform says something in French, realizes by the dopey look on my face that I haven't a clue, and switches to English. Her parade of pretty words turns out to mean Good evening miss, let me help you. She opens a door and hands me a towel—cloth, not paper.

The toilet has a real seat, not the black horseshoe kind, and a lid with a present on top wrapped in light blue paper. When I open it, it takes me a minute before I realize it's a toilet seat cover so I won't catch germs. Even the flush sounds expensive—a quiet waterfall instead of a whoosh.

The sink has a crystal bowl full of guest soaps like the ones in our hotel in Phoenix. You use one, then toss it. After you dry your hands, you put your towel in a white wicker hamper, and if going to the bathroom wears you out, there's a bench covered in the same material as the couches in the other room, and more magazines.

I hand the lady the dollar, and on my way to the door, I try out one of the couches to find out what being rich feels like. It feels like me sitting on a couch, so I leave.

Outside the restaurant, there's a row of horse-drawn carriages parked at the curb.

"How about it," Mr. Stephens says. "Would you ladies like a tour of Old Montreal?"

I say yes the same time Mama says no.

"You've spent enough," she says. "This is too much."

"You let me worry about that," he says, helping her into the first carriage.

The horse is dressed for a party, and the driver looks like the coachman in *Cinderella*. He hands Mr. Stephens two blankets. He tucks one around me and the other one around my mother and himself. I'm sitting opposite them, and right here, I decide that this is the last date I'm coming on. How is this romance supposed to get off the ground with Manny in Mama's head and me watching over them like a dumb chaperone?

Once we're on our way, I lock my head in a sideways position and wrap my thoughts around Eva. I haven't seen her for two weeks, not since Halloween. She won't come to the phone when I call, and every time I go to her house, her mother says she's in bed. It's probably the flu. Maybe tomorrow she'll feel better. Come back then.

Sadness seeps into my heart like a cloudy day, and the clip clop of the horse's hooves on the cobblestone streets hypnotizes my mind and keeps the gloom frozen there.

* * *

Sirens wake me in the middle of the night and I sit straight up on my cot. The wailing stops so near I think that maybe our house is on fire. Mama stirs on the couch and says it's probably an ambulance for old Mrs. Parsons down the street. She's ninety with a bad heart, poor soul. Go back to sleep.

CHAPTER SEVENTEEN

—◆—

MR. STEPHENS IS IN THE back of the classroom watching as our student teacher bungles his way through a lesson on the first Thanksgiving. You can tell that he's making up stuff as he goes along and trying to remember what he learned in second grade. It wouldn't surprise me if he whips out construction paper and has us make pilgrim hats and Indian headdresses. His eyes are bloodshot and he has a gigantic hickey on his neck—fresh.

We're the last stop before he's released into the world to get a real teaching job. If I were Mr. Stephens, I would say, *Okay, loser, hold it! Stop right there.* Then I would draw a great big zero minus on the board and tell him that's his grade and he should look for another line of work—bartender, maybe, or gigolo.

The kids are so bored that the room is in motion with bodies shifting in chairs and feet scraping the floor. The new boy who took Madeline's place is carving his name into the seat of his chair with his jackknife. The girl in front of me has fallen asleep on her desk and is making soft snoring sounds. I start counting to a hundred so I won't explode from the frustration that's rising inside me. Just as I hit ten, the fire alarm takes pity on us and grants us a reprieve. Even Mr. Stephens has a look of relief on his face when he takes back the helm. "Okay, everybody, single file. You know how to act during a fire drill." He signals the student teacher to turn off the lights. He grabs our coats.

We're the first class out the door, and when I see Dr. Singer's car pull into the parking lot, I think that Eva's better and he's bringing her to school. She'll think we all came out to welcome her back—a colossal homecoming. He gets out of the car alone and walks toward Mr. Stephens slowly as if it's an effort to lift his feet. He says a few words and hands him a note. Then they both look at me—concerned.

When I see the desperate hurt in Dr. Singer's eyes, I suck in my breath and pull my belly toward my backbone tight. The thought of why he's here paralyzes my brain and I stand planted to the ground. Then the siren from last night blasts in my head. The ambulance—it didn't come for old Mrs. Parsons at all. She's at home alive right now with her bad heart still beating, drinking a cup of tea and watching soap operas. It's Eva who's dead.

Mr. Stephens comes over and says that my mother has given permission for me to go with Dr. Singer. He rummages through the pile of coats the student teacher is holding until I point out mine and then he helps me on with it. "You go along now," he says, cupping the back of my head in his hand, looking hard at me with sorrow in his eyes.

The front yard of the school is overflowing with kids now, laughing and breaking the no-talking rule. The flag in the middle of the lawn is snapping sharply in the wind, and I think how the janitor will soon be sent out to lower it to half-staff out of respect for the dead. The line of kids in my class is quiet and they watch me walk toward Dr. Singer as if they're looking at a car accident, curious but respectful, and at the same time, happy that it's not them.

Dr. Singer holds the door open while I get in the car. Then he closes it easy like he doesn't have the strength to do it the regular way. When he gets in, I notice that his hair isn't combed and he hasn't shaved and he's wearing mismatched clothes that look like he slept in them—nothing like his regular put-together self. "I'm sorry for pulling you out of school, Beth," he says, like I'm one of his patients and he's breaking the bad news about my test results. "Eva's in the hospital and she keeps asking for you. She's having a real hard time and you're the only one she wants to see."

This is like when you're dreaming that you're drowning. There's nobody there to save you and your insides are in a panic and you're going down for the last time, but then you wake up. Tears burn my eyes and quiet sobs grab my chest and force it into motion. A huge lump wraps itself around my throat and makes me feel as if I'm being strangled. She's not dead. She's just in the hospital—with the flu probably. Thank you, God, for letting her not be dead.

"She tried to kill herself last night." Dr. Singer pushes the words out of his mouth slow and heavy like boulders.

A timid sound escapes my mouth. I look over at his dead brown eyes and think how easily a person's soul can disappear. "Will she be okay?" I ask, trying to get my brain around what he has just told me.

"She's not going to die if that's what you mean."

* * *

Mrs. Singer is standing outside Eva's room. Her face is white and there are sunken black marbles where her eyes used to be. She smiles weakly when she sees me, then pulls me close and hugs me so tightly and so long it's as if she thinks she'll fall into a hole if she lets go. I feel the hardness of her belly pushing into my front and I think of the perfect baby that's growing inside her—the one that can't possibly be as perfect as Eva. She loosens her hold on me, cradles my chin in her hand, and tips my face up so our eyes are connected. "Do you know what's happened?" she asks in a whisper.

I nod, want to look at the floor, but she's holding my face so that I settle my eyes on the plaid collar of her shirt.

"Did she say anything to you about why she's so unhappy?" she asks, touching my cheek like a soft breeze. She gives me a beseeching look and waits for an answer. I shake my head, but say nothing. "We tried for weeks to get her to talk about what was bothering her, but she wouldn't say a word. She just stayed in her room and wouldn't see anybody." She looks over at her husband and says, "We should have taken her to somebody. I don't know what we were thinking. I thought it was just a phase and she'd get over it. My God . . . what are we going to do?"

She speaks so deeply from her heart and she's in so much pain that my words give themselves permission to come out of hiding. I have to do it fast before my brain says No! "It's the baby," I hear myself say. "She thinks because she's not good in school that she's a disappointment to you and you're trying to replace her with the baby. She thinks you want to send her away to school to get rid of her, so she won't embarrass you anymore."

"Oh." The word comes out as a moan—like she's been beaten nearly to death and that's all she can say. She backs against the wall, covers her mouth, and her glare pierces me like a knife. I return her gaze, then look away.

Dr. Singer puts his hand on my shoulder as tender as anything and says, "Why don't you go in and see her now. She's been waiting for you."

As I reach for the doorknob, I look over at Mrs. Singer and think how a person's happiness can be chipped away as quickly and easily as old paint.

Eva looks so small it's as though the bed has swallowed her whole. The dark of her hair stands out stark against her colorless face, and the white of the bandages that are wrapped around her wrists matches everything else in the room. She watches me walk toward her, and when I'm standing next to her, she looks straight at me. Tears fill her eyes and spill over onto the pillow. "Pretty stupid, huh, Beth? I couldn't even do this right." I can't think of anything to say, so I sit on the chair next to the bed and wait. "I didn't really want to die," she says. "I just wanted to take a break from my life for a little while, give my parents a break."

"They don't want a break," I say. "They just want you to be okay."

"I know that." She cries huge now. I take hold of her hand and wait until she can talk. "I can see what I've done to them, what it would have done to them. I don't know how I could have been so selfish. I'm so embarrassed. Damn it, Beth, hand me a Kleenex."

"At your service," I say, relieved to hear a little of the old Eva coming back.

"Did you see the bars?" she asks, blowing her nose and pointing her face toward the window. "I'm on the goddamn mental ward. I have to stay here a whole week and the only way they'll let me out is if I start seeing a shrink full time."

"That doesn't sound so bad," I lie, thinking I'd rather die than have to do that.

"Not for you, maybe. You don't have to do it."

"Well . . . if you hadn't done such a dumb-ass thing, you wouldn't have to go either." The words slip out before I can put on the brakes. Now that I see she's going to be all right, a rage builds inside me and shoots straight out my mouth. "You already know what you did to your parents. Well, how do you think I felt when I thought you were dead? You're my best friend. I love . . . I care about you. If you ever decide to do that again, call me first. I'll do it for you."

She looks at me, lowers her eyes, says nothing.

"I'm going home now. I have homework. I'll come back tomorrow." My hard-hearted voice surprises me.

* * *

That night I have a dream that Eva and I are angels in heaven dressed all in white with huge fluffy wings. We both have bandages on our wrists. She kisses my wounds, then I kiss her full on the mouth. This wakes me up and I have the same amazing feeling down deep inside that I had the day we met. I try to get to sleep again fast so I can crawl back into my dream, but it doesn't work. All that comes is sleep—plain.

CHAPTER EIGHTEEN

—◆—

THE WEATHERMAN ON THE car radio is telling us that we'll be having a white Christmas this year. Well, no joke. I wonder how many years he had to go to weatherman school to figure that one out. All you have to do is look out the window to see that there's a blizzard going on.

"It's coming down an inch an hour," the radio guy says. "By nightfall there'll be a foot or more." I think he used the wrong instrument for that one. He should have used my grandfather's hat. There's already an inch of snow on the brim and he's only been outside for fifteen minutes. He's got the earflaps down and tied under his chin like a little girl's Easter bonnet. Besides, the snow is way past the top of his galoshes, and they're nearly up to his knees, so we've hit more than a foot already. It's so cold out that his nose is the color of strawberry jam and his breath is rolling out of his mouth like rivers of smoke.

I look at him and think how old people can get away with wearing stuff like earflaps and goofy-looking boots and long scarves tied around their chins like toddlers. People expect it. If anybody not old went around looking like that, they'd be asking for it. I wonder who's in charge of making up rules like that. God, probably. I think it's His way of giving old people a break. They have enough to deal with without having to worry about what to wear.

We're on our way to get a Christmas tree and we're stuck in a snowbank. Grandpa's putting on tire chains and I'm minding the car like he asked me to, which just means that he's afraid I'll get hit by a truck or something if I get out, plus he doesn't want me to get cold. I think how he pours his whole wonderful heart out onto me, all the good stuff he's been storing up for years, because my grandmother has shut him out and won't accept it.

While I'm waiting, a snippet of jealousy pinches my heart when I think how Eva has fallen in love with her psychiatrist. "His name is Steve," she tells me after her first visit. "It's really Dr. Hudson, but he wants me to call him Steve, can you believe it?" I make my face look as if I'm thrilled for her. "Beth, he's major handsome, fall over on the floor good looking and not old either, right out of college, I think."

"Wow!" I say, wondering what his wife looks like and where his kids go to school.

"I think he has a crush on me," she gushes.

I send my real thoughts to bed without any supper and say, "Wow" again.

"He even keeps me longer than my hour . . . well, really fifty minutes because they have to have time to rest between patients. When the timer rings, he doesn't pay any attention. He just lets me go on talking until I've finished what I have to say."

I think how she's like a newborn puppy—all blind and needy.

"He told me I'm one of the most interesting girls he's ever met, maybe he said the *most* interesting, I can't remember."

"That's great," I say. And here is what I say to her in my head. *Give me a break. He gets paid to say things like that. Twenty-five dollars a pop!*

"And look," she says, holding out a piece of paper. "He even gave me his own personal answering service number in case I need him after office hours. All I have to do is call, and he'll call me right back."

I feel like grabbing that paper out of her hand and smacking her over the head with it for being so naive. "That's really nice of him," I say. "He sounds terrific."

"He's dreamy, that's what he is. I can't wait for a week to go by so I can see him again. I just have to think up some really sick-sounding stuff to say so he'll keep making me come back."

My brain is tapping its foot. "That's good," I say. "I'm glad you like him."

"*Like* him! He's absolutely—"

"Well, dolly, we're ready to go," Grandpa says, holding the car door open and stamping the snow off his boots. "This thing's like a Sherman tank now. We'll be able to plow through anything. I should have put the chains on before we left, but I didn't realize it was going to be this bad."

"Maybe we should wait until tomorrow," I say, in case that's what he wants to do but doesn't want to disappoint me.

"This is the first Christmas tree we've had since your mother left," he says with a smile. "We're going to get it today before your grandmother changes her mind. Besides, the plows are out now. We'll be fine."

When we get to the Christmas tree farm, Grandpa takes his axe out of the trunk and we head for the field. "Just a minute," he says, propping the axe against his leg. "Come over here a minute. I don't want you sick in bed for Christmas." He pulls the hood of my jacket up over my head, ties it securely under my chin, and gives it a pat. "There you go," he says as I look around to see if there's anybody important who might see me looking like an idiot. We're the only ones here, so I follow him, thinking how much warmer I feel. "There's a beautiful Scotch pine right there," he says, pointing to the first tree we come to.

This is the only Christmas tree I've ever had, so I'm going to make sure it's perfect. "That one's nice except it's got a hole on this side," I say, circling it ready to find fault. I realize that the hole could be turned to the wall and nobody would see it. But *I* would know it was there and it would be spoiled.

"You're right. I didn't see that," he says. "There are plenty more over there. Let's go take a look."

*   *   *

While we're in the farmer's kitchen paying for the balsam fir that Grandpa tied to the top of the car, the farmer's wife says, "Looks like you got a touch of the frostbite on your cheeks there, mister." I look over and see white circles where his rosy skin used to be.

"Here, dolly, let me look at you," he says, holding my chin in his hand and tilting my face toward his.

"Ah, you don't have to worry about her," the woman says. "These young kids can stay out all day. Their blood still works. Maybe yours will be okay," she says, running her finger around Grandpa's white circles. "It hasn't turned black yet. Don't put anything on it, no warm water or anything. Just let it thaw out by itself. That'll be five dollars. Cash, no checks."

Well, now I feel just awful. I made my grandfather traipse around for an hour and now his face is going to fall off. "I'm sorry, Grandpa," I say when we get to the car and he's giving the tree a wiggle to make sure it's fastened securely.

"Sorry for what, dolly? What did you do?"

"I made you stay outside so long your face froze."

"Don't worry about that. I can't remember when I had such a good time. That old buttinsky doesn't know what she's talking about. I've had frostbite before and this isn't it. Some people just like to look at the dark side of things."

Well, if this isn't the perfect time to ask him about my grandmother, I don't know when would be. I wait until we're back on the road headed home and then I say, "Has my grandmother always been unhappy?"

He waits so long to answer I think he's thinking I'm a buttinsky too. "No, dolly. When we were first married she was happy. You should have seen her. She was the sweetest little thing . . . just like a porcelain doll."

"What happened?" I ask, surprised.

"Life happened. I happened."

I look over at him, but say nothing.

"Your grandmother came from a very wealthy family. They lived down by the lake in a mansion. Judge Spencer bought it after her parents passed."

He stops talking and I think that's all he's going to say.

"Is that all?" I ask. "That's why she's unhappy?"

He shakes his head and sighs. "She married me against her parents' wishes. They didn't think I was good enough for her and I guess they were right." The heater is blasting us with cold air, so he turns it off. "Anyway, they died in a hotel fire in New York City soon after we were married and they left everything to her brother. That was her punishment for marrying me. I couldn't support her the way she was used to, and little by little, she came to resent me."

"What about Mama? Didn't she ever love her?"

He looks over at me with a pitiful attempt at a smile. "Your grandmother loves your mother. She just has a strange way of showing it. Her parents pampered her when she was little, so she wasn't used to having to tend to things herself. Her family always had help and we couldn't afford it. She had a hard time being a mother."

"She doesn't have to take care of Mama now."

"No, but she had big plans for your mother just like her parents had for her and things didn't turn out the way she wanted them to. Sometimes you get disappointed when you try to live your life through somebody else."

"Yeah, I guess," I say, thinking that's a flimsy excuse for the way my grandmother behaves.

*   *   *

By the time Mama gets home from work and my grandmother comes down from her nap, we have the tree decorated like a princess dressed for a Christmas ball. Mama carries on something fierce until finally her face turns into a puddle of happy tears. I see the tiniest bit of a crack in my grandmother's veneer—almost a smile—a memory maybe of a happy Christmas long ago, before life betrayed her. I take a chance and think that maybe things are headed in the right direction.

CHAPTER NINETEEN

———•———

IT'S CHRISTMAS EVE and I'm in church sitting between Grandpa
and Mr. Stephens—sentries protecting me against the world. My
mother is playing the piano, and my grandmother is standing in
the choir loft singing *O Holy Night*. Her voice is so clear and true
that shivers are chasing each other up and down my arms.

She's the regular soloist, so I'm used to hearing her sing, only
tonight is different. The church is full. The Christmas and Easter
people have crawled out of the woodwork and have filled the
pews to overflowing. Pyramids of flaming poinsettias donated
by people in memory of their dead relatives dress up the altar,
and a Christmas tree decorated by the Sunday school classes
stands by the organ, all white light glittery. Also, it's dark and
cold out, so everything seems cozy—like how hot chocolate
feels after you come in from being outside too long, and every
part of you is frozen solid.

My heart is so full and I feel so holy that I imagine God has
come down from heaven and is sitting on my lap. Plus, there's
a whole pile of presents under our tree at home with my name
on them.

After the sermon, the preacher tells us to bow our heads in
silent prayer. He instructs us to remember the sick and the poor,

the hopeless and the helpless. I take a chance that enough other people in the congregation are taking care of those pitiful souls, and I put every second I've got into one prayer, which I repeat until my time is up: *Please God, let Mr. Stephens ask Mama to marry him tonight.* When the preacher calls time, I picture God, still sitting on my lap, but looking like John Wayne now. He's glaring at me with disgust on His face. He waggles His finger at me and says, *Lots of luck with that prayer, little lady.*

After church, Mama goes off with Mr. Stephens to a party at Ralph and Bertie's, and my grandmother, Grandpa, and I go for a ride to look at Christmas lights.

"You sounded really good tonight," I say to my grandmother from the back seat. I'm hoping that a tiny bit of Christmas spirit has entered her stone cold soul.

She shifts in her seat and clears her throat.

"You're right, dolly," Grandpa says. "Your grandmother has the voice of an angel."

Nothing from her. A sigh of defeat from him. He finds a radio station that's playing Christmas carols, and while he drives slowly up and down the streets of Ridgewood, I take myself back a week to Eva's piano recital.

* * *

I'm sitting in the high school auditorium with her parents, joining in the cooing as we watch a parade of adorable baby beginners plunk out their ten-second ditties. Some of the kids are so tiny that the teacher has to help them onto the piano bench. When the middle-size players begin, the pieces get longer but not much better, and the audience turns on them for being not so cute and not very good. The oohs and aahs stop and the whispering and coughing and squirming begin.

I glance over at the Singers. Dr. Singer, dressed like his perfect handsome self, has his hands clasped in front of his face like a praying mantis and is watching the performer as if he's the official adjudicator. Mrs. Singer is wearing a blue checked maternity top over her dress jeans. She pats my knee and gives me a smile—her regular jocular self. There isn't a hint of the falling-apart, panicky people I saw that day in the hospital, and they haven't said anything to me again about what happened.

When the advanced players begin, the audience gets even antsier. Now we're into the not-so-good pieces that go on forever. Some of them have stops in the middle where we're not supposed to clap, but not everybody knows that. At first, there's solo applause from different parts of the auditorium until we all catch on and sit on our hands.

There's a horrible break in the whole boring thing when a timid-looking high school boy dressed in a too-big tuxedo comes out, sits down, steals a peek at the audience, and freezes with his hands perched above the keys. He stays poised there like a statue, and the longer he sits, the quieter the audience becomes until the silence booms like a bass drum. Finally, the teacher has to come on stage and lead him off, defeated.

I feel so sorry for him and think how terrible it will be if that happens to Eva. I've never heard her play and I'm already embarrassed for her having to be on display before all these people. I look over at her parents sitting there so calmly and feel angry at them for making her do this. Don't they know that she feels stupid enough without having to be humiliated even more? I look at the program and see that she's next. She's the last one to play. She must be dying back there. The piece that is printed by her name, *Prelude in C# minor by Rachmaninoff*, is hard enough to read. I wonder how she's going to play a thing like that.

Eva steps onto the stage dressed in a raw silk blouse and a long hunter-green velvet skirt—the outfit she bought when her mother took us to the fancy boutiques on Sherbrooke Street in Montreal. Her dark shiny hair is wrapped on top of her head in a knot like a ballet dancer, and the stage lights are doing the jitterbug on the diamond studs in her ears, the ones her parents gave her last week for her fourteenth birthday.

The audience gives her its attention just because of the way she looks—like Natalie Wood at the Academy Awards. She stands by the piano, scans the audience until she spots us, and smiles just a bit before she sits down. She takes a little time adjusting her skirt and getting comfortable. Then she begins to play.

Well, this is where my jaw drops onto my lap. I can forget about worrying that she's going to make a fool of herself. She's playing this piece as if she wrote it. The heavy massive chords flow through her fingers and out the open mouth of that piano with such deep, rich tones the audience is mesmerized. My body relaxes. There's no way that she's going to make a mistake. So *this* is where her genius lies. This is why her parents were so confident. I look over at them and see pure pride on their faces. Mrs. Singer glances at me with tears in her eyes. I smile at her and she takes my hand and holds it until Eva is standing by the piano bowing. Then we both join the audience in clapping until our hands hurt in appreciation of her talent. I think I might burst wide open because of the love I feel for this girl.

* * *

I wake up before Mama on Christmas morning, and because I'm still groggy, the realization of what I see arrives slowly, like a sunrise. But there it is on her finger—sparkling to beat the band. I wonder how she can lie there asleep when something this exciting has happened in her life. I owe God a lot for this one. I'm in such a good mood, I feel like dancing.

CHAPTER TWENTY

MAMA AND I ARE ON the bunny slope at Whiteface Mountain. Mr. Stephens is teaching us how to ski. He gave us Head skis and White Stag outfits for Christmas, the real McCoy and brand new, not secondhand stuff like we're used to. Mama has reached her goal weight and she looks really good in her black stretch pants, light blue parka, and matching earmuffs. Mine is navy stretch pants, white parka with navy trim, and a really great alpine hat with braided ties, which of course you don't tie, otherwise you'll look like a dunce. Eva clued me in on the fashion part of this whole thing and she thinks that Mr. Stephens has fantastic taste. She came with us and is schussing down the hard trails waiting for me to get good enough to ski with her.

"You're a natural, Elizabeth," Mr. Stephens says in his regular positive way. "One more time down the bunny hill and then I'll show you how to use the chair lift. You'll do fine on your own."

I can tell he'll be spending most of the day trying to get Mama past the snowplow, but they're both having such a good time I don't think he cares. Even though she still reads Manny's letters once in a while, she seems to be genuinely crazy about him. The wedding is planned for August and she has asked me to be her

maid of honor. She wants a church wedding with lots of guests
because she and Manny got married by a justice of the peace
and it was chintzy and cold with borrowed plastic flowers and
nobody there but strangers.

*   *   *

Mr. Stephens and I are standing in the chair lift line with a
bunch of rich-looking people and I'm thinking so *this* is how
the other half lives. Then I realize that I'm here with all my ritzy
stuff, so I must be other half too.

I feel proud knowing that everyone around me probably
thinks that Mr. Stephens is my father, and how nice my future
is going to be because of him. He bought a lot on a new street
near our school and he and Mama have been spending most
of their time looking at house plans. The one they settled on
is a three-bedroom ranch with two full baths. As soon as the
ground thaws in the spring, the builders will start. I can hardly
stand how excited I am about having my own room. I've waited
my whole life for this.

For some strange reason the laundry lady from Phoenix comes
into my head, and I wonder if she'll have to spend the rest of
her life folding other people's underwear and cleaning up after
slobs who make the washers overflow and leave coffee rings on
the tables. I think how nice it would be if everyone could have
a Mr. Stephens.

*   *   *

After my chair lift lesson, I see Eva at the bottom of the mountain
talking to a boy—a good-looking boy. My reaction catches me
off guard. I'm so overcome with jealousy that my insides turn
on me. The pit of my stomach contracts and my heart starts
beating so fast it's as though someone is playing it like a bongo
drum. Then a panic fills me like no other I have ever felt before.

Dark ugly thoughts invade my brain and I picture myself beating that handsome boy over the head with my ski pole.

"Hey, Beth, you're doing great!" Eva yells when she sees me. "Come here a minute. I want you to meet somebody."

"Oh, okay," I yell back. I point myself downhill and head toward them with my mind full of revenge. Instead of stopping the right way, I make believe I'm a complete incompetent and snowplow into what's-his-name's skis. "Ah jeez," I say, looking down at the scratches my steel edges have put on his brand new Rossignols. "I'm sorry. I'm not so good at stopping yet."

"That's okay," he says with a genuine smile on his face. "They needed to get broken in. Now I won't feel like such a dweeb. My name's David Franklin. Eva's been telling me all about you. I guess we moved here about the same time."

Well, honest to Pete, this just isn't fair. How's a person supposed to hate somebody this nice?

"David lives in Ridgewood," Eva says. "He's in high school, a freshman. His father's a colonel at the air force base."

"Oh," I say, not caring one tiny bit about what she's telling me.

"I'm having a party Saturday night," he says. "Mostly base kids, but you two are welcome to come."

"We'd love to," Eva says fast without even looking at me. "What time?"

"Eight o'clock. It's the big Tudor house at the end of Hanover Lane. You can't miss it."

"Can you believe it?" Eva squeals as soon as he's out of earshot. She's squeezing my wrist with the strength of a weight lifter and holding her chest as if she's about to fall over dead. "The base kids are so cool," she says with a faraway look in her eye. "I hear they're like three years more mature than the townies. Finally, we'll get to meet some boys who have stopped playing with their Lincoln Logs."

"Oh good," I say, thinking how much I don't want to go to this party.

"Isn't he gorgeous?"

"Who?"

"Who do you *think*? Sometimes you're just so damn dense. David Franklin. Isn't he just sex on wheels?"

"You mean skis," I say with no enthusiasm at all. "He's okay, I guess."

She rolls her eyes big time. "Honestly, Beth! We're going to have to jumpstart your hormones, if you have any. Sometimes I wonder."

"My hormones are just fine, thank you very much. Come on. Let's go skiing. That's what we came here for, isn't it?"

CHAPTER TWENTY-ONE

"YOU HAVE TO BEND over, grab everything you can find, and stuff it in," Eva says while she's showing me how to make breasts by pulling my stomach and the skin under my arms into a push-up bra. We're in the dressing room of the JC Penney lingerie department trying to fix what nature forgot. "There, that's not too bad."

"How's it going to stay there? This is stupid. Let's just forget about it. I don't care if I go to the party or not." I stand up and all our hard work disappears.

"Shit, Beth," Eva says, stamping her foot hard. "Sometimes I worry about you. This is our big chance to meet boys. If you're going to wear one of my sweaters, you've got to have something to put in it. Otherwise, you might as well stay home and watch Lawrence Welk with your grandmother. Boobs are what boys look for first in a girl. If you had even a *little* something to begin with, we wouldn't have to work so hard. Cripes! My Uncle Ira's got more up top than you do."

"Forget about your uncle," I say, feeling like killing her. "How am I supposed to keep my stomach from falling out of my bra?"

"When we get home we'll duct tape it. We just had to see if this would work. I think it'll be okay. It's either this or falsies. You can't trust falsies, though. They like to travel, they're like little Gypsy boobies. They don't call and let you know when they're leaving, either. You could end up flat-chested and humpbacked and not even know it."

"*Very* funny," I say, handing her the bra and putting my undershirt back on. "How come *you* know so much about fake boobs anyway?"

"It's not from personal experience, smartass. I went to camp with a girl who wore them and they were always getting away from her. One day we had a mixer with the boys' camp across the lake and her falsies floated out of her suit and went swimming by themselves. A couple of the boys played water polo with them and ended up wearing them on their heads for the rest of the day. Believe me, duct tape is a lot safer. All it does is rip your skin to shreds when you take it off."

This throws her into a giggle fit and she crouches on the floor and starts jiggling around like crazy. "Honest to God, Beth, I can't stand much more of this. I'm going to pee my pants as sure as anything. Just *buy* the damn thing and let's get out of here."

"Give it to me!" I say, wanting to strangle her with it. "I'm never coming shopping with you again as long as I live."

* * *

We stop by Majors for ice cream sodas on the way home. When Mama comes to take our order, Eva turns into Miss Goody Two Shoes. "Hi, Mrs. McMann," she says like butter wouldn't melt in her mouth. "It's so nice of you to let Lizzy spend the night at my house so she can help me with my school project. You must be really proud of her being so smart and all."

"She's a winner," Mama says, all chirpy like she's been since her engagement.

"Yeah, she's a regular genius," Eva goes on. "I wouldn't be able to do this assignment without her and it's very important. It's due on Monday, so we have to get it done tonight. We'll probably be up terribly late, and we'll have to sleep in tomorrow. I'm just really glad you're letting her come."

"That's okay," Mama says. She raises one eyebrow and tilts her head like there's something rotten in Denmark, but she's not sure what it is.

I give Eva a kick on the ankle to shut her up. I feel bad enough about lying to my mother. If she keeps this up, I'm going to have to start answering questions about what I'm really going to be doing tonight. There's no way Mama would allow me to go to a boy-girl party.

Eva's parents think it's terrific. Since her incident, they pretend that everything she wants to do is hunky-dory. Like if she said, *I would like to parachute off the Empire State Building*—they would say, *Of course, dear, that sounds like a wonderful idea.*

"I bought the new undershirts you sent me for," I say, holding up the bra bag hoping to change the subject. All this lying is making me lose my appetite for the soda Mama's making.

"That's good," she says. "Maybe next time we'll get you some training bras. You're getting to that age."

"That's what *I* wear," Eva lies, sitting there in her black lace underwire push-up with matching panties. "You have to teach those little buggers how to behave before you put them in the real thing."

Well—now she's done it. If there's one thing Mama can't stand it's sass—especially sexy sass. I wait for her to have a stroke and then to tell me I'm never allowed to see Eva again. When she starts to laugh, *I* nearly have the stroke.

"That's a good one, Eva," she says, putting our sodas in front of us. "Teach them how to behave . . . honestly, you're a stitch!"

My brain has to take a deep breath and ponder what it has just witnessed. I think how Mama has changed for the better since Mr. Stephens and Bertie came into her life. The best part of the whole thing is that she calls my grandmother *Mother* now and she lets her mean remarks roll right off her back.

"This soda's great, Mom," I say, taking a long thirsty drag on the straw.

"It sure is," Eva says. "They're really going to miss you here after you get married."

Mama stops wiping down the counter and leans against it. "You know," she says, "I'm going to miss working here. The people are really nice, but John wants to take care of me. He's going to buy me a piano like the one I used to have so I can give lessons at the house. It'll be nice."

"I didn't know about the piano!" I say, licking the last of the chocolate off my straw.

"I didn't either," she says, "not until last night, and you were asleep when I left for work this morning."

"That's great," I say, thinking how everything in our lives is turning out so right.

"Well, I guess we'd better go to my house and get started on that project," Eva says, dusting her mouth with her napkin.

"I suppose," I say, unable to look my mother in the eye. "'Bye, Mom."

"'Bye, Lizzy. Have a good time at the party."

Well, this is one of those awful times when you don't know what to say or where to look. I freeze like a bank robber who's been caught before he's even left the bank. I wait for the handcuffs to be slapped on.

"Eva's mother called to tell me she'll be dropping you girls off and picking you up. She checked around and found out that the Franklins are nice people. Very religious, born again even. She didn't want me to worry."

I'm not sure where this is leading.

"Enjoy yourselves. But, Lizzy . . . "

"Yes?"

"Next time tell me. Okay?

"I will," I say, thinking how lucky I am to have her for my mother. "I'll see you tomorrow. And, Mom . . ."

"What?"

"I'll be home in time for church."

She smiles, shakes her head, and goes back to wiping the counter. Half of me is wishing she had told me I'm grounded forever and that I'm forbidden to go to boy-girl parties for my entire life, but the other half doesn't want Eva to go without me.

* * *

"I'll be waiting right here at ten o'clock," Mrs. Singer says while we're getting out of the car in front of David Franklin's house. "I'll be in my bathrobe so don't make me go to the door. Oh, and girls, be polite to Colonel and Mrs. Franklin. I hear they're lovely people, but rather formal. Be on your best behavior."

David Franklin answers the door with a beer in his hand. I look over to see Eva's reaction. Her face says, of course he's holding a Budweiser. What else would he be doing? But, I know her well enough—she's just as shocked as I am.

"Hi there," he says, toasting us with the bottle. I can tell by the look on his face that he has no idea who we are—Fuller Brush ladies, maybe. I wish I could tell Eva what I'm thinking. Let's go home now and play dolls and drink hot chocolate in our jammies.

"Hi, David," Eva says, clueless about the question mark he's wearing on his face.

"Hi," he says back. Maybe we're collecting for the Red Cross.

"I am really *so* sorry about those scratches I put on your skis," I say, thinking if this doesn't do it, we might as well ask him if he'd like to make a donation to the March of Dimes and leave.

"Oh, yeah! Hi!" he says. "Come on in."

Well, this house is movie star fancy—Persian rugs, velvet couches, real paintings, a huge basket of fresh flowers next to the fireplace. I hear faraway music. *Runaround Sue*.

"Where should we put our coats?" Eva asks.

"Oh, just throw them on that chair over there," David says, chugging the last of his beer.

Eva takes hers off but I say, "I'll keep mine on for a while. I'll just unbutton it. I'm still a little cold." I'm thinking about my homemade breasts and how they look more like I'm hiding small animals under my sweater than the real thing. This is one of those situations where you wonder what on earth you were thinking about when you agreed to do it—like you've been in a coma and you wake up and have no idea where you are or how you got there.

"Come on, the party's downstairs," he says, leading the way.

"Are your parents down there?" I ask.

"That's a good one," he says with a laugh. "Sir and Yes Sir are safely out of the way in Baltimore, some religious retreat, and I'm here all alone reading my Bible like they told me to."

He looks back to get our reactions.

"That *is* a good one," Eva says.

"Sure is," I say.

We look at each other wide-eyed, and I think how sad our parents are going to be when our pitiful mangled bodies are discovered.

The downstairs looks as if this is where Dick Clark tapes *American Bandstand*—real jukebox, hardwood dance floor, soda fountain. The room is quiet for just a second and then Gene Pitney starts to sing *Only Love Can Break A Heart* and the people on the dance floor entwine themselves around one another and start swaying in place to the music.

"Help yourselves to refreshments. There's beer in the fridge," David tells us, and then he's gone to gather Marilyn Monroe in his arms and join the swarm of lovers on the dance floor.

"Take off your coat for God's sake," Eva whispers in my ear. "You look mental standing there dressed for a snowstorm. You're still wearing your mittens for crying out loud."

"Why don't we call your mother to come get us," I say, thinking how much over our heads we are. "We can go to the movies or something."

She glares at me as if I have said, *Would you like me to stick a nail in your eye?* Before she has a chance to say anything, a Frankenstein-looking guy grabs her hand and pulls her toward the dance floor. He towers over her by a foot, and he wraps her up so tightly, I can only see from her waist down. Just as I'm watching him slide his baseball glove hand over her butt, a tall, regular-looking boy asks me to dance.

"Do you want to take your coat off?" he asks nicely.

"Oh, that's okay," I say, stuffing my mittens into the pocket. "It's not very heavy."

"Suit yourself," he says, shrugging his shoulders. Then he takes my hand gently and leads me onto the dance floor.

I wait for him to tell me his name and ask me mine when he pulls me close and slides his hand inside my coat. I can feel his hard *thing* press into my stomach and then his hand is on my tiny mouse boobs. His sweaty cheek is pressed against mine and I hear a chuckle in my ear, but I have taken my brain home to the attic. I have my back against the warm chimney and I'm reading *Heidi* or maybe *Rebecca of Sunnybrook Farm*. Mama's there too, reading her letters. Every once in a while she looks at me and smiles. The music stops and he asks me if I want a beer. In my mind, Mama is asking if I would like some milk and cookies.

"No. Yes. I don't know," I say. "What are you asking me that for? Why do you want to know?"

He looks at me as if I should be wearing a straitjacket and leaves—fast.

Before I know how I got there, I'm upstairs sitting in the living room with a river of tears running down my face because of the shame I'm feeling. How could I stand there and let him grope me like I was a cantaloupe he was checking out to see if it was ripe before he bought it?

I'm thinking how I am nowhere near ready for the world when Eva comes running into the room.

"What a bunch of creeps!" she says, wiping her mouth with the back of her hand. "I've got to find a phone."

While we're waiting on the front porch for her mother to come she says, "This makes me want to give up boys forever."

"Yeah," I say, "me too."

CHAPTER TWENTY-TWO

———◆———

TODAY IS MY BIRTHDAY. I'm a bona fide teenager. I take a long hard look at myself in the mirror to see if turning thirteen has magical powers attached to it—a presto change-o kind of thing. Nope. Nothing. Just the same reflection I see every morning. As I stand here inspecting my face, a heavy feeling of impending doom invades my brain, and I wonder where that came from—probably just me being a jerk. I try to shake it off, but a tiny piece lingers like an annoying mosquito that just won't leave.

Mama took me shopping for clothes yesterday, and this morning at breakfast she gave me a silver bangle bracelet and a year's subscription to *Seventeen*. Mr. Stephens is going to take the whole family out for pizza tonight and then to Howard Johnson's for cake and ice cream. He wants me to call him John now, only not in school because it wouldn't be fair to the other kids. After the wedding, he's going to adopt me and then I'll call him Dad. The word sounds so special when I try it out in my head, like it's gold plated. I know he'll have something super nice for me like always. I'm hoping it's the portable radio I've been hinting about, the one with the real leather carrying case from the Sears catalog.

When I stop at Eva's to pick her up for school, her mother answers the door wearing a party hat. She slaps one on me and sings *Happy Birthday,* even the *How old are you now* verse. Although she has more than a month to go before the baby is due, her stomach is so enormous it looks as though it might explode at any minute.

"Well, how does thirteen feel?" she asks, cradling my face in her hands, scrutinizing it. "I don't see any wrinkles."

"Fine," I say, forcing a smile. "It feels fine." I wish I weren't such a failure at small talk. I hope Eva hurries up.

"I got you a little something," she says, scooping a small present off the coffee table and handing it to me.

I can tell she put a lot of effort into the wrapping—peach flowered paper with a matching bow, brand new, not left over from Christmas like we do at home.

"Go ahead, open it," she says when she sees me standing there gaping at it.

"Oh, okay," I say, picking at the Scotch tape like I'm a surgeon performing a delicate operation. I haven't had much practice with the unwrapping part—not until Ridgewood. In the other places we lived, Mama would take me to a store the day before Christmas or my birthday and let me pick out something. She made sure it got put in a bag, but that was it. The only presents she wrapped were Manny's. Then she fussed over them like crazy making sure everything was perfect. When she'd hand him one, she would stand there with a pitiful look of anticipation on her face. He'd plow into it like a bulldozer, and in a second, all her hard work would turn into a pile of rubbish on the floor. I never heard him say he liked anything she ever gave him, and I think it would have killed him to say thank you.

"Just rip it," Mrs. Singer says excitedly impatient. I can tell by the expression on her face that if I don't get a move on, she'll open it for me. "I just love to see people open presents," she says, holding out her hand for me to give her the wrapping. "I hope you like it."

I take the cover off the square white box and inside I find another box—black velvet. "Oh!" I say when I open it. "It's beautiful. I love it. Thank you." It's a gold circle pin with my initials in script. The tentacles of the letters are entwined around each other like best friends not wanting to let go. I know this is *real* gold, fourteen carat, because Eva has one just like it. She wears it all the time.

I hug Mrs. Singer as much as her belly allows, and her face tells me that she loves me. Not the same as a daughter, but close.

"Do you like it?" Eva asks on her way down the stairs. "Let's see."

I open my coat and show her where I've pinned it to my sweater.

"Well, you don't wear it *there*," she says, dropping her books on the floor and rescuing me from myself. She unpins it and moves it a quarter inch to the right.

"It has to be *directly* below the point of your blouse collar. There, that's better." While she's inspecting her work, her mother and I give each other looks that say Eva's the fashion expert. We might as well go along with her because she won't stop harping about it until we do. She puts on her coat and picks up her books. "I have something for you too," she says, "but I'm going to make you wait until after school. Oh, by the way, happy birthday!"

Well, if this isn't my bonus day. It's not even eight o'clock in the morning and I've already had enough good things happen to last a whole year.

*   *   *

Now, *there*. My luck has turned on me. I knew things were going along too smoothly. The gym teacher who took Mr. Brand's place has gotten it into his head that we should learn how to dance.

"All right, everybody," he barks out like he's talking to a bunch of marines, "boys on one side, girls on the other. Come on now, let's hustle."

He's a short, round bald guy named Mr. Pine and I think he stays up nights thinking of ways to torture us. Last week it was rope climbing and the week before that he made us do a whole period of calisthenics.

"Why do we have to wear our gym suits if all we're going to do is dance?" one of the popular girls whines.

"What class is this?" he asks, fingering his whistle.

"*Gym*," she says, like the spoiled brat I'm sure she is.

"Does that answer your question?"

She gives him an *I'm going to tell my mother on you* look and sashays back to her cronies.

I think how things have changed since Mr. Brand left. He used to treat the athletes and the cheerleader types and Madeline with kid gloves. The rest of the class might as well have stayed home. I like how Mr. Pine is fair. He hates everybody the same.

"All right. Face each other and no moving from your spots and I don't want to hear any complaints," he says after he's gotten our attention with a blast from his whistle.

"Okay. Now, boys, move forward slowly. Girls, stay where you are."

I'm on the end and I can see where this is leading. Yup—I was right. Not enough boys.

"You on the end," Mr. Pine says, looking straight at me, "stay right there. *I'll* be your partner."

Oh, goody, I think. Just what I was hoping would happen. Wait until I tell Eva this one. She'll bust a gut.

Mr. Pine walks toward me blowing his whistle. When the class is quiet, he takes my hand and leads me toward the center circle on the gym floor. "All eyes here," he says needlessly because where else would anybody be looking? "I'm going to demonstrate the correct way to hold your partner."

Oh, my Lord! Please, God—let me die right here. I don't care about the rest of my birthday. Just kill me now.

"Okay, boys, place your right hand just below the girl's left shoulder blade like so," he says, turning me toward the class

so nobody misses the fact that his old man hand is in the correct spot on my back. "Then take your partner's right hand in
your left, like so." I'm just about to ask if I can be excused to
go to the ladies' room when he says, "Now watch this." Before
I have a chance to open my mouth, I get pushed around and
stepped on. "Front together, right together, back together, left
together. That's all there is to it. That's the box step. It'll get
you anywhere you need to go as far as slow dancing. All right
now, take hold of your partners and we'll do it once together
before I start the music."

Finally he sets me free and heads toward the record player by
the door. I follow on his heels, look him straight in the eye, and
say what Eva says works every time with men teachers. "Mr.
Pine, I need to go to the nurse. I'm having female problems."

"Oh, well, um, why sure. Go!"

While I'm changing, geriatric music wafts into the locker
room. I sit on a bench and wait for the class to be over. I think
how Mr. Pine probably doesn't want to teach us how to dance
any more than we want to learn. I'm sure it's part of the cur-
riculum he has to cover in order to get his paycheck. I guess
even teachers have to do what they're told.

* * *

On my way home from Eva's, I'm carrying my very first diary
and my beautiful green marbled Esterbrook fountain pen with
the bottle of turquoise ink—necessities she calls them. I'm going
to wait until after my birthday dinner to start writing my secret
thoughts so I can include every single thing about my special
day. I'm nearly home and I'm wondering who owns the old
junk heap of a car that's parked in front of our house when I
see the Arizona license plate. God doesn't pay any attention to
the prayer I keep repeating, because when I open the front door,
Manny says, "Hey, kid. Long time no see."

CHAPTER TWENTY-THREE

———◆———

I'M NOT SPEAKING TO GOD. Since Mama went back to Phoenix I have not said one single solitary word to Him. If I weren't so scared that He might do something even worse, I would give Him a piece of my mind like how He should be ashamed of Himself for messing around with people's lives just when they're going in the right direction. How hard could it be for Him to look down and say, *All right now . . . those folks look mighty happy. I guess I'll just leave them alone and go whip some criminals into shape.* My grandmother still makes me go to church, but when the preacher starts in with the God stuff, I pretend the inside of my head is a jukebox and I listen to the top ten.

Punxsutawney Phil saw his shadow today, so we'll be having six more weeks of winter. Mr. Stephens is doing the groundhog lesson himself since we have a new batch of student teachers that aren't ready for anything more than lunch and recess duty. I can tell that he's feeling the same as I am. He makes his face look normal and smiley, but I know underneath that mask there's a mountain of pain.

I have rerun the events of that horrible day so many times in my head that my brain is worn down to a nub. When I walk into the living room, there is Manny sitting on the couch with his feet crossed in front of him on the coffee table. My grandmother hasn't come down from her nap and Grandpa is still at his store. Mama, who's supposed to be at work, is kneeling on the floor putting things into her suitcase. "Oh, Lizzy. Hi," she says when she sees me come in the door. "Manny came to see us. Wasn't that nice of him? He has a new car. Did you see it? He drove all the way from Phoenix."

I stand there dumbstruck, watching as my life is smashed to smithereens.

"Lizzy," Mama says, "did you see it?"

"What?"

"Did you see Manny's car? It's right out front. *Lizzy!*"

"No. I didn't see it."

Manny sits up, puts his feet on the floor. "Kid," he says, "your mother's coming back with me. When we get settled, we'll send for you. We have to find a place and all. Will you get me some coffee? Instant's fine if that's all you've got."

I look over at Mama, but she doesn't look at me. She closes the suitcase and stands up.

"Hey, kid, how about that coffee."

"I thought you got married," I say. "I thought you married Sylvia Bushey."

"Oh, that," he says, "that one didn't take." He walks over to my mother and rubs his hand across her bottom. "Those young kids are too hard to tame. I'm better off with the tried and true." He goes into the kitchen and starts searching through the cupboards. "What's a guy got to do to get some coffee around here for crissake? Here's some instant. Kid, make me a cup of this."

I try to kill him with my eyes. "Mama," I say, "what are you doing?"

"I have to go, Lizzy. I love him. We'll send for you in a couple of weeks. I promise."

"Where's my coffee?"

"We'll get some coffee on the road," Mama says. "I got paid today."

He slams the cupboard doors. "Well, let's go then. I need some goddamn coffee."

I stand there like a stick while Mama tries to hug me. I smell perfume on her neck, the Tabu Mr. Stephens gave her for her birthday. "It'll be okay," she says. "I'll send for you. You'll see. It'll be fine. And, Lizzy, will you give this to John for me?" She hands me an envelope. I can feel a note and the engagement ring—our future stamped *Return to Sender*. "I'm sorry I don't have more time. Say goodbye to Mommy and Daddy for me. Be a good girl. I'll see you soon."

As I'm watching out the front window, I can hear my grandmother's footsteps on the stairs. "What's all the racket down here?" she says annoyed as she walks toward me. She looks out the window in time to see Mama and Manny getting into the car. "Oh, dear Lord," she says. "I was afraid of that." The words come out slow and heavy and her shoulders droop. She looks at me, opens her mouth to say something. Instead, she heaves an enormous sigh and goes back upstairs.

* * *

The attic is cold, and even though I still have my coat on, I wrap myself in Mama's blanket, sit next to the warm chimney, and stare at the empty rocking chair. I won't have to take the cot down tonight. I'll sleep on the couch with her pillow.

I wonder how a mother can choose a man over her own daughter. A wild animal wouldn't even do that. I think what I would do if I had to choose between Mama and Eva. I would choose Mama. That's the way it's supposed to be. I guess she doesn't know that rule. I think how close I came to having Mr. Stephens for my father. Tears stream down my face and a lump fills my throat that's so huge I can't swallow. Cross off my life.

———

CHAPTER TWENTY-FOUR

Dear Diary,

It's been a month since Mama left and we haven't heard a word from her—not even a collect call. She said she would send for me. Ha! That's a good one. I would never go back to live with Manny in a million years anyway, but I would like to have the satisfaction of saying so. They would have to drag me by the hair screaming all the way and then I would hitchhike right back here to Eva. I could have gotten run over by a car by now and be dead and buried and my own mother wouldn't even know. I think I hate her.

Mr. Stephens took me out for spaghetti last night. It was served with garlic bread and a green salad topped with Italian dressing and bacon bits—real, not the fake ones. When he asked if I wanted spumoni for dessert I said, Oh sure, like I'd had it a million times before. It turned out to be really good. Pink and chocolate ice cream with cherries and pistachio nuts. Next week we're going for Mexican. Something called tacos. I will say I like them even if I don't. I wonder what Mama's eating. Bread and water, I hope.

My grandmother is taking things pretty well. I guess she's decided that living her life through my mother doesn't work.

*I think she has all her hopes pinned on me now. She'd change
her mind real fast if she knew I was in love with a girl. Plus, I'd
be out the door on the end of her foot. Good thing this book
has a lock on it!!!*

*I have to stop now. Eva and I are going to the movies to see
To Kill a Mockingbird. I loved the book so much I hope they
don't mess up the movie like they usually do. After that, Dr. and
Mrs. Singer are taking us out for michigans and then I'm going
to spend the night at their house. I've never had a michigan
before, but they're Eva's favorite—hot dogs with spicy sauce
invented right here in Ridgewood.*

*Everybody is treating me like I have a terminal disease
because of what's happened. I wish things were back the way
they were, but what good does wishing do. More next time.*

* * *

"With or without?" the waitress asks, looking straight at me
with her pencil poised above her order pad.

"With or without what?" I ask.

"Onions. Do you want your michigan with or without?"

"With, please."

"Buried?"

"Pardon me?"

"Do you want your onions buried?"

"Buried where?"

She looks at me as if I'm the biggest bonehead she has ever
come across. "Under the hot dog. Do you want your onions
under the dog or on top?"

"Under."

"So you want them buried."

"Okay."

"Do you want French fries or onion rings?"

"Sure."

"Which *one*?"

"French fries."

"Something to drink?"

"A chocolate milkshake please."

"Regular chocolate or black and white?"

"What's black and white?"

She swallows hard and rolls her eyes so huge I expect them to fly right out of her head. "Chocolate syrup and vanilla ice cream."

"Yeah. That sounds good. I'll take that."

She presses down on the order pad with such force that her pencil lead breaks. "I'll be right back," she tells Dr. Singer and walks away mumbling.

Eva and her parents start laughing so hard the whole booth shakes.

"Thanks a bunch for clueing me in to this stuff before we came so I wouldn't make a fool of myself," I say, feeling so much a part of this family that my heart is brimming with joy.

"We're sorry," Dr. Singer says, wiping the tears off his face with his handkerchief. "It was just too sweet to stop."

When the waitress comes back, Dr. Singer says, "Three more of the same please."

She looks at him like she'd love to punch his face in. "You couldn't have told me that before I left?"

"Sorry," he says, fairly composed.

When she brings our food, everyone is on his best behavior. The giggle fit has passed and we're trying to make up for our rudeness, and *she* knows that tip time is right around the corner and Dr. Singer looks like he probably has big bucks in his pocket. "Thank you," we each say in turn as she places our plates in front of us.

"Enjoy your meals," she says with an authentic-looking smile. "If there's anything you need, my name is Sue."

"Thank you, Sue," Dr. Singer says, "but I think we're all set here."

Well, now I know why Eva likes michigans so much. These things are fantastic. I can see why they're the official food of Ridgewood. I wish Mama could taste one.

* * *

It's almost eleven o'clock when Dr. Singer comes in Eva's room and shakes us awake. "We have to go to the hospital," he tells Eva. "The baby's coming. I'll drop you off on the way, Beth. It could be a long night. We'll call you tomorrow and let you know what it is."

* * *

I'm still awake when the front door opens and Mama comes in. I play my deep sleeping act to the hilt as she comes over to the couch and kisses me on the forehead. Her lips are so cold and her body gives off such a chill that she must have walked all the way from the bus station. She goes upstairs to the attic and I expect her to come back with the cot. Instead, she heads toward the kitchen and goes out the back door.

I tiptoe up the stairs and look out the round attic window into the backyard. The street lamp on the corner lets me see her dump Manny's letters into the burn barrel and light a match. I watch as the tiny flame springs to life and devours its dinner. The last to go in are the candy box and the faded blue ribbon. She stands and watches as her past is reduced to dying embers and then disappears entirely. Cross off Manny forever. Thank you, God.

By the time she comes inside, I have my cot set up and a cup of hot tea waiting for her. She lets me help her off with her cold things and put on her warm nightie—the flannel one my grandparents gave her for Christmas.

I sit down next to her on the couch and put my hand on hers. "I'm glad you're back, Mama," I say with such a feeling of relief that I didn't know until now how scared I was that I might never see her again.

She looks at me, sighs, and pulls me over to her. "Oh, Lizzy, sometimes I think you're more the mother than I am. What did I ever do to deserve you?"

"Just lucky, I guess."

She shakes her head, gives me a closed-mouth smile. "I promise I'll never do anything like that again. I'm so sorry. I don't know what I was thinking."

"That's okay. Let's go to bed. It's almost tomorrow."

I wait until she's settled on the couch and then I turn out the light. As soon as my head touches the pillow, the anger I feel toward her for being so selfish hits me like a bomb.

"Lizzy, how's John?" she says, trying to be so cool—like she's asking about the weather.

"He's fine. He even takes me out to eat and to the movies."

"Really?"

"Oh, sure. Next week we're going for Mexican."

"What do you two talk about?"

He asks me every time I see him if I've heard from you and I lie and tell him that you call every day so he won't know what a lousy mother you are. "Oh nothing. Just stuff."

"What kind of stuff?"

"Regular stuff."

"Does he ever ask about me?"

"No."

"Oh. I was just wondering."

That should shut her up.

"Did you give him the ring?"

"Yeah."

"What did he say?"

He didn't say anything. He just sat there wounded. Like a puppy that had been kicked in the head. "He said thanks."

"I wonder what he'll do with it."

"Probably give it to Marlene."

"Who's Marlene?"

Nobody. I just made her up. "Oh, just some lady he's always talking about."

That did it. Not another word from her. She deserves it. She has to learn that she can't go around butchering the hearts of the people who love her and get away with it.

* * *

When my grandmother comes down, I actually enjoy watching as Mama gets her comeuppance. Even Grandpa gives her serious what for. This time she really screwed up. Nobody messes with *his* baby granddaughter and gets away with it. I would like to chime in and describe, or at least *try* to describe, the overwhelming disappointment and anguish she's piled on my heart. But when I see the agony on her face and the way her body sags and has lost its will to live, I know she realizes that she has painted herself into the corner of my grandmother's wrath just as solidly as she had the first day we arrived from Phoenix. This time, though, I can see my grandmother's point of view and it makes me feel like a traitor. If only Mama could get her head on straight. The way it is, she'll always be her own worst enemy.

CHAPTER TWENTY-FIVE

WELL, EVA IS CRAZY ABOUT her baby brother. All I hear is Peter this and Peter that. I think how she nearly went nuts because she thought he was going to take her place, and now she thinks he's the greatest thing ever!

I have to admit he really *is* sweet. So tiny and helpless. He doesn't look like a magazine baby. He's not round and cuddly yet; he's more like how kittens are before they fill out and turn cute. He has twig arms and skinny bowed legs that stiffen straight out when he bawls his head off because he's hungry or wet or who knows what—just because that's all he knows how to do, I guess.

That's another thing, the way babies cry. As if they come equipped with fire alarms and they can break the glass and pull down the handle at the drop of a hat. I think God did that so they wouldn't be put in corners and forgotten. It's that kind of thing that makes me sure He's really up there. The fact that He filled in all the blanks—right down to the tiniest detail.

Being around Peter makes me think what *could* have been if Mama hadn't fallen into Manny's trap. Maybe she and Mr.

Stephens would have had a baby. I'd love that and I would never have to worry about being replaced, even though the baby would be his own flesh and blood, because I know he's still crazy about me. He doesn't take me out to dinner anymore, but he makes up excuses to keep me after school to make sure everything's okay. I can tell he's still in love with Mama too because he asks me a million questions about her, but I think he's been hurt so deeply and he has too much pride to go begging for another chance.

I have my fingers crossed for a miracle though, because today is parent conference day. Mama took time off from Major's and she's at school right now picking up my report card. She's never gone before because I always get mostly A's, so she doesn't see the point.

I take my mind back an hour and replay the nervous breakdown I nearly give her while she's getting ready for her appointment.

"Can you see any holes?" she asks, standing in front of the sun-streaked window gently patting her teased hair.

"Yeah . . . one big one," I say as sarcastically as I can.

"Where?" she asks, rushing to my grandfather's dresser and grabbing a hand mirror. "I don't see anything," she says, turning in circles inspecting her beehive. "Where is it?"

"Your *hair's* fine," I say. *"It's your head that's got the hole in it."*

"I just asked you a simple question. Why are you being so snotty?"

"I was just kidding. Sorry."

"Look, Lizzy, I feel terrible about what happened, but I can't undo it. People make mistakes every day."

Not like this one. Only a moron would throw a gem like Mr. Stephens away and go crawling back to an astronomical loser like Manny McMann. "Yeah. I guess."

"You won't understand until you're grown up. Love's a funny thing. It makes you act crazy sometimes."

Well, I can't argue with that, but let's see how she lies her way out of this one. "What happened anyway? Why did you come back? Did Manny find another bimbo?"

"Of course not! How can you *say* such a thing? He *begged* me to stay." She looks over to see if I'm buying it. My face tells her I'm not. "I got lonesome for you, if you want to know the truth. Besides, Ridgewood is a much better place for you to grow up. In a real house and all."

Oh, *please.* Give me a break. I *know* kids are supposed to love their mothers no matter what, but she really makes it hard sometimes. "This isn't our house," I say with as much gall as I can muster. "We're not even welcome here."

Silence from her. I know I could finish her off with a few more digs, but it wouldn't be a fair fight, so I back off.

"So do you want me to tell you how to get to my room?" I ask in a civil voice.

"No, that's okay. I know where it is. John took me there once when he had to pick up a book. Do you think he's still seeing that Marlene person?"

"Who?"

"Marlene. The woman you told me he's always talking about."

"Oh, her. I don't know." Well, now, here's how a lie sneaks around and bites you in the backside. I'd forgotten all about old phony Marlene.

"Does he still talk about her?"

"Not very much."

"Do you think they're still going together?"

"I'm not sure, but I wouldn't say anything to him about her. It might make him feel uncomfortable."

"You're probably right. Do I look okay? Is this dress too tight?" she asks, running her hands over the hips of the double-knit coral sheath with the bolero jacket—the one that cost so much she put it on layaway before she left for Phoenix and just picked it up today. "I'm so nervous about seeing him I'm actually shaking. Look at my hands."

"You look fine," I say in a mother's voice. She looks more than fine. Since her Phoenix disaster, she's lost even more weight and she looks almost like her prom picture, only modern.

"Well, here goes nothing," she gives her hair another douse with Aqua Net and picks up her purse and gloves from the bed. "Wish me luck."

I'm even more anxious than she is about this meeting, so to make the time pass faster, I go to Eva's and help her baby-sit Peter while her mother is at her six-week check-up.

"You are *not* going to believe what he just did!" Eva says as soon as she opens the door.

"What?" I ask, expecting her to tell me about one of his many colossal diaper accomplishments.

"He said *Eva.*"

I screw my face into a picture of disbelief. "Oh," I say, "*really.*"

"No, really, it's true," she says, nearly in a panic. "Come on. Maybe he'll say it again."

We stand next to the bassinet in the family room waiting for Peter, who can't even control his eyes yet, to start talking.

"Eee-*vah.* Eee-*vah.*" She prompts him.

Peter lies there slurping on his fist.

I get in her face and exaggerate a fake yawn.

"Never mind then!" she snaps. "He's a genius. I know he is. He just won't do it because *you're* here."

When I see how upset she is, I feel terrible and try to make it up to her. "Yeah. You're probably right. He's obviously just tired of saying it. Did you know that Einstein talked early like that, but he would only do it for certain people?"

"Yeah . . . I heard about that."

Well—now we're both lying because I read that Einstein didn't talk until he was three. "Why don't we take him for a walk? It's nice out."

"Okay, but I have to change him first. My mother fed him just before she left."

Mrs. Singer is so open about breast-feeding. She doesn't think anything of whipping one out any old time. Peter roots around like a baby pig until he finds the faucet and then he clamps on and makes the most satisfied little noises—like he's been wandering around in the desert for days and has happened upon an oasis.

* * *

Peter is asleep in his carriage and Eva and I are on the swings of the campus school playground when I see Mama come out the door. I can tell by how her head is down and the way she's walking like somebody died that she botched it.

"Isn't that your mother?" Eva asks, making figure-eights in the sand under the swing with the toe of her shoe.

"Yeah," I say, half disgusted and half so disappointed that I could burst into tears right here.

"Aren't you going to say hi?"

"Nah . . . I'll see her when I get home."

"I guess it didn't work," she says, shaking her head and making clucking noises with her tongue.

"What didn't work?"

"Well, just *look* at her. You can tell she's a woman on the prowl. She put too much effort into it. She should have acted more blase, like she was only there to get your report card. She tried too hard. Men don't like that."

I look over at Eva, and I'm sure that she's exactly right, but some sort of cockeyed loyalty grabs me by the throat and I pounce to Mama's defense. "What do *you* know about it anyway? What makes *you* such an expert on the subject?"

"Well . . . I . . . "

"Oh, just shut up! At least *my* mother *tries* to look nice."

Well, now I've done it. I don't even know where that came from. Eva's face turns into pure hate. She leaps off the swing and pushes the carriage so hard over the bumpy playground that

Peter lets out a startled scream. I run to catch up with her, grab
the handle to stop her. "I'm sorry. I didn't mean . . . "

"*Get* your hand off this carriage." Her jaw is clenched hard
and the words come out single file and powerful like they would
make dents if they hit a steel building.

"Please, Eva . . . just listen."

"Get *away* from me. You're such an idiot. I never want to
see you again."

I watch as she heads home, her body stiff with indignation. I
keep my eyes glued to her and hope that she looks back because
that would mean she still cares at least a little, but she doesn't.
When she's out of sight, I sink back onto the swing and blame
Mama for destroying my life. I wish for lightning to strike me
dead—or a heart attack.

When I have run out of evil thoughts, I remember the lot
Mr. Stephens bought for our new house. To put off having to
breathe the same air as Mama, I walk toward what-could-have-
been with gloom following me like a shadow. When I get there,
I sit on the huge rock where my bedroom would have been. I
know this because he told me when he brought me here. "And
this is where *your* room will be, Elizabeth," he said, so happy
and excited I thought he might break into song. "You have the
southeast corner so yours will be the sunniest. You'll have to
think about how you want it to look, what kind of furniture
you like."

My insides dry up and shrivel into nothing when I think how
many times I decorated that room in my head before Mama
slithered back to Phoenix and took my future with her. I have
a good eye for what goes together. I don't think you can learn
a thing like that—not really. You're either born with it, or
not—like it's a gift. I've never told anybody this, not even Eva,
but I'm going to be an interior decorator when I grow up, have
my work in *Architectural Digest*. I have to wait until I have a
place of my own so I can prove myself. Then people will look
at it and say, *You did this—by yourself?*

Mr. Stephens' car door must have made a noise, but I didn't hear it because when he says my name, I jump. "I'm sorry. I didn't mean to scare you."

"Oh, that's okay," I say—an intruder caught red-handed. "You didn't scare me." I get off the rock fast because it's not mine anymore. I don't belong here.

"What are you doing?" he asks. His face is plain. I can't read it.

"Oh, nothing. Just . . . nothing."

He sits down on his rock. "Care to join me?"

I smile only with my mouth—my face does not participate. "Okay. I guess so." I surprise myself because I'm a little angry with him and I know I shouldn't be. He didn't do anything. It's just that I didn't do anything either—it's all Mama's fault. She should have to take the full punishment, but in this case it doesn't work that way because I'm part of her.

He dusts off a spot next to him with his hand and gives it a pat, waits for me to sit down. He's dressed up today for the parents, I guess—new tan suit, polished brown shoes, nice tie, the same cologne he wore on his first date with Mama. I think how pretty she looked and I picture the two of them together on the top of a wedding cake.

"So," he says, "who's Marlene?"

I don't look at him. Instead, I stare at how the starched cuff of his shirt digs into the skin just above his watch—Timex with a brown leather band, new. I bite my bottom lip so hard I taste blood.

"So-o-o?" He bends his face down to meet mine and looks into my big teary eyes.

I shrug, staring at my hands. "Nobody" slides out of my mouth sounding as pitiful as the word itself.

"They'll be starting to dig tomorrow," he says, picking up a handful of dirt and letting it sift through his fingers.

"Dig?"

"The cellar for the new house."

"Oh." That's why he sent Mama packing. He's found somebody else. I'm sitting in some other girl's bedroom. The realization of what has happened plows into me hard—knocks the wind out so I can't breathe. I have to get away from here. I stand up to run, but he grabs hold of my hand.

"Will you do me a favor?" he says, reaching into the inside pocket of his jacket. "Will you give this to your mother?"

He hands me back my life, and my face turns into a sloppy mess of tears. Inside the envelope I can feel a letter and the engagement ring and he doesn't seem to mind that I wet his new jacket when I hug him.

"You didn't think I was going to let *you* get away, did you?" he asks as if he's talking about a chest full of diamonds. He takes his handkerchief out of his pocket, holds it to my nose, and tells me to blow.

"But why didn't you tell her yourself? I saw how sad she looked when she came out of school."

"I thought I should make her wait a little—at least an hour. I didn't want her to think I'm a pushover." He tweaks my chin and smiles. "Besides, you delivered the bad news. I thought it was only fair for you to be the one to put things together again."

I think about the ways people are so different—how there are the crooks and the murderers and the Mannys. Then the Mr. Stephenses and the Mrs. Singers come along and more than make up for the losers.

I sit back down on my rock and feel relief pump through my body like a transfusion. "I was afraid you wouldn't give her another chance," I say, "after what she did."

"She had to do what was right for her."

"But she didn't even tell you she was going."

"Elizabeth, you have to be patient . . . give a person room to breathe. Some things are worth waiting for." He sits down next to me, puts his hand on mine. "Your mother had to work out the wrinkles in her heart in her own good time. She had to close one door in her life before she could open another one. I'm giving her another chance because good people deserve at least that much. Besides, I love her . . . I'm just glad she came back."

"Me too."

"I was on my way to your house when I noticed you here," he says, standing up and brushing the dirt off his pants. "Do you want a ride home?"

"Sure," I say, holding out the envelope. "I can't wait to see her face when I give her this."

*　*　*

Mama still has her gloves on and she's clutching the handles of her purse with both hands, the same as she did the doughnut bag in Phoenix. She's in the chair next to the round window staring straight ahead when I walk into the attic.

"Well, how did I do?" I ask in a cheery voice.

"What?"

"My report card. Was it good?"

"Oh, yes. You did fine. Here it is, right here." She opens her purse and hands me the card.

I sit down with my back against the chimney and look at the row of A's. Then I read how I'm such a high achiever and dependable and kind to others and a pleasure to have in class and how he wishes everyone could be like me. I think how he really means it, not like some teachers who sugarcoat the report cards so they don't have to deal with unhappy parents. "So," I say, "how did it go for you?"

"How did *what* go?"

Oh, brother! We're going to have to go through *this* junk. "You and John . . . how did it go?"

"Fine."

"Fine how?"

"You know. We just talked."

"About what?"

"You, mostly."

Oh, sure—I really believe that one. "What about you two getting back together like you hoped?"

"Oh, that. I don't know. I've been thinking. Maybe he isn't the right one for me. I probably should take things a little more slowly . . . not fall for the first one to come along." She looks over at me. I nod. My face says that I think what she's saying makes perfect sense. "He really wants to get married, though. He put the pressure on something terrible, but I'm just not sure."

Oh, really? That's not what I heard. "Yeah . . . you're right," I say. "Somebody better is probably right around the next corner. Besides, you haven't known him very long. He could be a bank robber or a con man or maybe even a mass murderer. You can't be too careful about a thing like that."

This stops her dead in her tracks and she turns around and runs the other way. "What are you *talking* about? He's the finest man I've ever met. He's handsome and kind and considerate and as honest as the day is long."

"You think so?"

"Of *course* I do. What's the matter with you? I thought you liked him."

"He's okay."

She gets out of the chair, gives me a look that could kill, and heads toward the stairs.

"Oh, by the way," I say, "he asked me to give you this." I hand her the envelope and watch as she walks her fingers along it as if she's reading Braille. Her face comes alive like in the movie when Helen Keller unlocks the word *water*. Then she sits back down and opens the door to her new life.

After she has read the letter and put the ring on her finger, she clamps her hand over her mouth and squeezes her eyes shut so tightly that her brow furrows and her eyebrows turn into mountain peaks. Her silent sobbing makes her shoulders do push-ups and the feeling that wells up inside of me matches hers. I go over, put my arm around her shoulders and say, "He's waiting for you. His car is parked right out front."

"Oh, Lizzy," she says, as she locks my waist into a giant hug and rests her head on my chest, "I thought I'd lost him . . . made a mess of everything again. I don't deserve either one of you. You're both too good for me. You know that, don't you?"

I take her face in my hands and tilt it up toward mine. "Mama . . . you deserve the best. You just never knew it because nobody ever told you."

Big loud wet crying from her now.

I take her by the hand and pull her up from the chair. "Go!" I say. "He's waiting for you."

"I love you, Lizzy."

"I love you too, Mama."

After I hear the front door slam, the first thought that comes into my head is to hightail it to Eva's to tell her the news—and then I remember. I stand by the round window and stare at the red roof. A feeling of loneliness creeps over me and extinguishes the joy of what has just happened. I think how all the important things in your life have to be in tune or the whole song is ruined.

CHAPTER TWENTY-SIX

WELL, I CAN HARDLY believe it. I have what you might call a boyfriend. He's in my class and he's been buzzing around me since I came to this school. Until Eva and I had our falling out, I acted as if I didn't know he was flirting with me and he went away. Eva is an expert at carrying a grudge and I was so alone I thought what the heck—at least he's somebody to hang around with. Mostly we do homework together at the library and go to the drugstore for sodas, but tonight I have a real date. Dinner and a movie—*Under the Yum Yum Tree*.

Now, Robert Thayer is not the kind of boy that girls would drool over. In fact, and I feel guilty saying this, he's more the use him and lose him type. A puppet on a string. He likes me so much that he gave me a friendship ring, which is the big fad around school at the moment. This is supposed to mean that I am his girl and the other boys are to keep their clammy hands off. I keep it in my pocket when he's not around because it's the adjustable kind that bites. Besides, it's so cheesy it turns my finger green.

Mama answers the door when he comes and makes a big production about everything—taking pictures and all but bursting into tears because her baby is going out on her first date. If she knew what was in my mind—how I wish it were Eva picking me up for a date—she would put the camera away and save her film. Plus, she would have a complete nervous breakdown.

"Now, have a good time," she says all giggly as we're going out the door. "But remember, don't sit in the balcony."

Ordinarily, that kind of behavior from her would make me crazy, but because I'm with Robert and I don't give one tiny hoot about him, it doesn't bother me at all. In fact, she could come along with us and I wouldn't even care. After I said I'd go with him, I started beating myself over the head for being so stupid. The way it was, it was just two people doing homework. Going out on a date moves it up to a whole new level.

"We will," I say, "and don't worry about the balcony." Then I add, "I'll be home right after the movie," in case Robert gets it in his head to go for a snack or something. *Petticoat Junction* is on tonight and I'm not going to miss it.

Mr. Thayer is waiting in his car in front of the house and Robert opens the back door for me like his mother must have told him to. I'm hoping he sits up front with his father, but he slides in next to me—close.

"Well, Bobby," his father says, looking in the rearview mirror, "aren't you going to introduce me to your lady friend?"

Ah jeez, I think, why can't parents just be normal?

"Oh, yeah, I forgot. This is Elizabeth."

"I'm happy to meet you, Elizabeth," his father says, nodding his head like I'm the queen or something. "Bobby told me you were a looker, and he wasn't kidding."

Oh, for crying out loud. I feel like killing myself right here and getting it over with. What was I thinking? "It's nice to meet you too," I say, staring at the black elastic safety band he has holding his eyeglasses on so they don't fly off while he's doing something as dangerous as driving a car.

"I hope you like lasagna," he says, "because Mrs. Thayer has a piping hot pan ready and waiting. It's Bobby's favorite, right, Bobby?"

"Yeah, I like it."

"You've gotta hear this one, Elizabeth," Mr. Thayer says, slapping the knob he has attached to the steering wheel. "The first time he ate it he was two, maybe three years old. He couldn't say lasagna so he said ya ya, and he's called it that ever since. Isn't that right, Bobby? *Bobby?*"

Robert moves away from me defeated.

Okay, now I feel sorry for him because his father is such a jerk.

"That's the same with me, Mr. Thayer," I say. "I couldn't say spaghetti so I said sketty and I still call it that."

I look over at Robert and I can tell he isn't buying the lie, so I'm not going to try anymore. I just don't care enough. I think how he looks like a spoiled brat with his arms folded in front of himself tight and his lower lip stuck out a foot and his face frozen into a pout. Plus, how he has the top button of his shirt buttoned makes him look like a gigantic nerd. If you don't watch what you're doing, you can get yourself into a real jam. I think how my grandmother is making my favorite—stuffed pork chops—and how I'm going to miss *The Dick Van Dyke Show*, and I wonder when would be the best time to give Robert his ring back.

"So *this* is your little friend," Mrs. Thayer says when we walk into the living room—Danish modern. "I'm so happy to meet you."

"Me too," I say, wondering how Mr. Thayer could have landed such a beautiful, stylish wife.

"Why don't you show Elizabeth your room while I get dinner on the table," she says, giving Robert a peck on the cheek.

"That's okay," he says. "We'll wait here."

"Don't you want to show her your truck collection?" She looks at me and says seriously, "Bobby's got every truck Tonka ever made. All mint condition. We never let him play with them outside, of course, just on the carpet. He takes care of them like they're his babies, don't you, Bobby?"

Well, for Lord's sake. This just goes to show that some people shouldn't be allowed to have children. I think parents should have to pass some sort of test like you do for driving before they bring a kid into the world and wreck its life.

Robert follows his father's lead and helps me with my chair at the dinner table. He pushes it in so hard that my knees buckle and my arm knocks my water glass onto the red checked tablecloth.

Mrs. Thayer flies out of her chair like she's been shot from a cannon, runs to the kitchen, and returns with a roll of paper towels and a plain blue tablecloth. "Everybody up!" she shouts like she's the commander of a battleship. "Stand back while I clean up this mess."

I start to pick up my dishes so it will be easier for her. "No!" she barks. "Leave everything where it is. I'll do it. This is *real* china."

She's lying because hers is the same pattern that most of the housewives in Ridgewood have. The Grand Union is having a promotion: a dollar a place setting with a purchase of ten dollars or more. Made in Japan.

After she puts the Chianti bottle with the candle stuck in the top back in the middle of the table, we're allowed to sit down.

"I'm really sorry about that," I say, surprised because I don't feel sorry and I'm not one bit embarrassed about the whole thing.

"It's just that I like my dinners to have a theme," she says. "And, well, blue is *not* an Italian color."

"Right," I say, thinking how she must have one time been a little girl who was halfway normal—before she went nuts.

Then, without any warning, the parents grab hold of my hands and Mrs. Thayer says grace. After the amen part, the three of them cross themselves and Robert's mother looks at me and says as condescendingly as possible, "You're not *Catholic*, dear?"

"*No!*" I say as astounded as I can sound. "I'm a *Baptist*." Now, I don't really consider myself a genuine Baptist. In fact,

I wouldn't go to church at all if I weren't forced to. I'm more a person who feels that you can be just as close to God in your own backyard as you can sitting on a church pew. But, in this case, I'm glad I can throw in the Baptist part because of its shock value.

"Oh, I see," Mrs. Thayer says, giving her husband a look that says *we will be chopping* this *little romance off at the knees.*

* * *

When we get to the theatre, the movie has already started. I head for the middle, but Robert grabs me by the arm and leads me into the last row. "Why do you want to sit way back here?" I ask him. "There are plenty of good seats closer to the screen."

"I can see better from back here," he says, plunging his hand into the box of popcorn on his lap, not offering me any.

Just as I'm getting into the movie, I feel his arm creeping around my shoulders. "*Stop* that," I say. "I'm trying to watch the show."

He pretends he's deaf so I reach around, grab hold of his hand, and toss it back where it belongs. Before I can take a breath, his arm is around me and he's pulling me close to him.

"Cut it *out!*" I say in a loud whisper. I dig my fingernails into his wrist while I'm wriggling out of his grasp and throwing his arm in his lap.

"*I* paid for your ticket," he says in a whiny voice. "I ought to get *something* for it."

"I'll pay you back tomorrow. Just watch the show."

I'm thinking how pretty Carol Lynley is when he says, "Elizabeth?"

"What?"

"Do you want some popcorn?"

I turn toward him, and just as I'm saying, "Sure," he pulls my face into his and slithers his tongue into my mouth.

"You're such a moron!" I say, shoving him away. "Don't you *ever* try anything like that again. Stay here. I'll be right back."

I head toward the bathroom, and I can't believe it, but I actually have a tiny piece of his popcorn on my tongue. I wash my mouth out with the squirt soap that's attached to the wall, and then I use the emergency dime Mama put in my shoe to call my grandfather. While I'm waiting by the curb, I throw Robert's ring in the gutter and squash it flat with my foot.

"Trouble?" Grandpa asks when I get into the car.

"Nah—the movie just wasn't any good."

I know he doesn't believe me, and I think how sweet he is not to pry. When we get home, he makes popcorn and we watch *The Dick Van Dyke Show* together. Mama's out with John, so we have the living room to ourselves. I lay my head on his shoulder and I feel so safe and so loved I could start blubbering right here, but when Dick Van Dyke trips over that ottoman, we both laugh our heads off instead.

CHAPTER TWENTY-SEVEN

———•———

I GUESS MRS. SINGER IS sick and tired of Eva and me being mad at each other because she has taken the matter into her own hands. When she calls me to baby-sit Peter she doesn't let on that anything's wrong. "Are you free on Saturday, Beth?" she asks in her upbeat voice.

"Sure," I say, so surprised to hear from her that my heart does a back flip.

"We're going to a wedding and I was hoping you could take care of Peter."

"I'd love to," I say, "what time?"

"One-thirty would be fine."

As I return the phone to the cradle, the thought of seeing Eva puts a bounce in the step of my heart and I feel lightheaded—like when you first get off a whirly ride at the carnival and you have to hold onto something until your brain says, *Okay, I'm back.*

* * *

On my way to the Singer's, half of me is uneasy but the other half is so excited I have to pull back on the reins so I don't

break into a sprint. I wonder how Eva will act when she sees
me. Since our fight, we both go out of our way to pretend that
we're strangers. It makes me feel hollow inside—like I'm being
eaten alive.

Dr. Singer answers the door fumbling with his tie. "Hi there,
Beth. Mrs. Singer's in the family room feeding the baby. Go
right on in."

Peter is hanging over her shoulder like a dish towel and
she's pounding on his back making hollow thumping sounds.
"I'm glad you came early," she says, handing me the baby.
"I'm not even dressed. He's fed and changed, but he hasn't
burped yet, so see what you can do. I'll send Eva down with
the phone numbers of where we'll be. Oh, and there's breast
milk in the refrigerator if he gets hungry. You know how to
use the warmer."

I pace the floor massaging Peter's back and rehearse the lines
I've gone over in my head a thousand times. When Eva comes
in I'll say, *Oh, hi. You've had your hair trimmed. It looks nice
like that.*

I hear footsteps coming toward the family room and my
breathing decides to take a vacation. Dr. Singer walks in, hands
me a piece of paper. "We'll be at the temple for about an hour,"
he says, "and the reception after that . . . both numbers are
there."

"Is Eva here?" I ask. The words slip out sounding desperate.

"She is, but she's waiting in the car." He gives Peter a kiss
on his blond down-covered head. "See you, Beth. Thanks for
taking care of him. Remember to call if you need us."

Well, now I feel like a complete jerk—like I've been stood up
for a date. I was stupid enough to think that Eva would be happy
to see me, maybe even talked her mother into luring me here.

I walk into the dining room and stand back from the window
to peek out. She's leaning against the car with her eyes closed
and her face tilted toward the sun, which is making her new
flip shine like black satin. She's wearing a new dress—straight,

navy blue and white, cap sleeves. We always do her hair and clothes stuff together—she's the expert, but I'm there to agree with her.

My feelings are so hurt that I stare out the window and rub my cheek along Peter's head like a dejected housewife waiting for her unfaithful husband to come home.

I hear high heels on the stairs and see Mrs. Singer in a *dress*—light blue polyester, not pressed. "You look nice," I say, trying not to show my surprise.

"Thanks," she says. "I haven't worn one of these in so long I've forgotten how. I hope I remember to keep my knees together."

"You look gorgeous," Dr. Singer says, offering his arm. "You'll be the belle of the ball."

Mrs. Singer looks over at me and says, "I hope you and Eva land husbands as sweet as mine. He even lies with a straight face."

I smile, but don't know what to say. Peter changes the subject by letting out a thundering burp.

"Way to go, big guy," Mrs. Singer rushes over and takes him from me. "You *know* I don't want to go to this nasty old wedding and leave you behind." She lifts him over her head, gives him a wiggle and doesn't even mind when he spits up on her new dress.

"Do you want me to get you a soapy cloth?" I ask.

"No, that's okay. It's just baby perfume," she says, dabbing at the spot with the diaper from my shoulder. "I wouldn't feel complete without it." She nuzzles Peter's neck and hands him back. "Have fun with him, Beth. He'll probably be ready for a nap soon."

When they get to the car, Eva rearranges her mother's hair and tries to hand-iron the wrinkles out of her dress. Then, before she gets in, she looks directly at the window where I'm standing. I freeze, hope I'm a shadow. Then I watch Dr. Singer back down the driveway, and when the car is out of sight, my body relaxes.

I take Peter into the family room, rock him in the rocking chair, and pretend that he's mine. He looks up trusting me to know things and I feel so tender toward him that it makes me want to cry. I think how nice it would be to have a baby of my own who would love me, no matter what.

When he's asleep, I lay him on his stomach in the bassinet and head for Eva's room. Relief comes when I see that nothing has changed. I lie down on the bed, pull the covers up, and wrap myself in her scent. I run the last few weeks through my head and realize that I didn't fully realize until now just how empty I was without her.

You can fake your way through your life with a shield wrapped around your thoughts, pretending that everything is okay and that you don't really care. But when you let your guard down, your true feelings come rushing home to roost like a flock of ravens to devour your dead heart, and the loneliness of the whole thing barrels into you with such force you can hardly stand it.

I lie there with a river of gloom flowing over me when the thought of her diary floats into my head like a balm for my melancholy mood, picks me up from the bed, and takes me to her top bureau drawer. I'm surprised when I see it there because if I were her, I would have hidden it somewhere I could never find it. The fact that she trusted me to be a righteous person makes me feel ashamed and disloyal, but not enough to keep me from reaching to the top of the doorframe for the key.

I sit back down on the bed, and as I begin to break into the safe deposit box of Eva's life, my body comes alive with excitement. I'm about to find out what she really thinks of me and it fills me with a panic, the same as if a wild animal were coming straight for me.

* * *

I'm in the family room watching TV when I hear the front door open. I quickly check Peter to see that he's perfect, and then I sit back down on the couch and make my face look like it's interested in the show—*Planting Your Garden With Patsy.*

"I didn't think you'd be home for hours," I say when Eva comes into the room and drops onto the couch next to me. "Where are your parents?"

"They're on their way to the reception. I faked an upset stomach and they dropped me off on the way. Weddings have *got* to be the most boring things in the world. Unless it's your own, I suppose."

"You're right about that," I say, having no idea what I'm talking about because I've never been to one.

"The only boy there who is anywhere near my age is from my Hebrew class and a real creep. He always sits next to me close and whispers the answers in my ear and sprays his bad-breath spit all over me. I wasn't about to spend the next three hours with him draped over me on the dance floor. I'd end up dead—murder by drowning."

"Yuck," I say, thinking how one of us is actually going to have to look at the other pretty soon.

She takes her white gloves off one finger at a time and throws them on the coffee table next to her purse—new, navy, genuine leather.

"Nice purse," I say. "New?"

"Yeah. My grandmother sent me this whole outfit. She has great taste, not like my mother. I guess fashion sense skips a generation."

"Your mother always looks nice," I say.

"You're such a liar. You know . . . "

"Look," I say, "I'm really sorry about what I said. I didn't mean it. I love your mother."

"That's okay. I'm sorry too. I shouldn't have said those things about yours either. It wasn't any of my business. How's she doing?"

"She's getting married."

"No!" she screams, then covers her mouth with her hands. "You're kidding. She got him back?" She looks at me, grabs me by the shoulders, and shakes me hard. "That's great! My God, you must be thrilled."

"Yeah, I am. The house is even half finished."

"I saw that, but I thought maybe Mr. Stephens sold the land to somebody else."

"Nope, it's ours."

Peter either can't sleep with the noise or he's finished with his nap because he starts kicking his feet and making cute little baby sounds. Then he sets off the fire alarm.

"I'll get him," I say, partly because I'm not sure if I'm still on duty and partly because I love taking care of him.

"Okay," Eva says. "I'll go change and we can walk down and look at your new house. If that's okay with you."

"Sure," I say, thinking how absolutely perfect that is with me.

"Oh, yeah," she says, opening her purse. She takes out a five-dollar bill and hands it to me. "My father told me to give you this."

"This is way too much," I say. "I've only been here an hour."

"Just take it. He wants you to have it."

While I'm in the kitchen warming Peter's bottle, I think how Eva knows about me—that I love her in a way she could never love me back. I think how she knows, and she still wants to be my friend, and that makes her even more special in my heart—my heart that is so light and so full of happiness that I'm surprised I don't float straight up into the air.

———◆———

CHAPTER TWENTY-EIGHT

"HERE . . . HOLD THIS A MINUTE," Eva hands me her brand new overstuffed carryall, and runs a brush through her already perfect hair. School is out for the summer and her mother has just dropped us off at the city beach. We're standing on the tarmac by the concession stand, scanning the sand for good-looking guys—especially Greg Richards, Eva's latest heartthrob, a high school sophomore whose parents moor their speedboat at the same marina the Singers keep their sailboat.

Under my jeans and T-shirt, I'm wearing my bathing suit—last year's because it still fits, and if I bought a new one, I'd probably look for one just like it. It's a navy blue tank with crisscross straps. Plain. I have my rolled-up towel, a novel, and the portable radio Mr. Stephens gave me for my birthday.

Of course, Eva's suit is new: Rose Marie Reid lavender drape-front, strapless with the matching cover-up and petal bathing cap. Her shoulders are peeling badly from when she was working on her base tan and fell asleep under the sun lamp.

"Oh my God! There he is . . . don't look," she whispers, lowering her head and using her eyes as a pointer.

"You mean the dark-haired one who's asleep on his stomach and couldn't see us if his life depended on it?" I ask.

"*No*," she says, spitting the word at me like she can't believe I could be that stupid. "That's his friend. Greg's the blond one looking at the water."

"Well, either way . . . "

"Come on," she says, grabbing my arm and heading for a spot where anybody who wants to go to the bathhouse or the concession stand will have to walk right by us, two blankets down from lover boy.

She makes a big production of shaking her beach towel before she smoothes it out on the sand. She takes off her cover-up, folds it neatly, and drops it in my lap. Then she wipes nonexistent sand from her legs before she sits down.

"Is he looking?" she whispers, without moving her lips. A ventriloquist.

When I turn my head to check, she snaps at me through clenched teeth. "Don't look!"

"Well, how am I supposed to . . . "

"Never mind, you'll ruin everything."

Out of the blue, she starts laughing—loudly. Then she says, "I can't believe you said that!" She uses her ventriloquist voice to tell me to act like we're having fun.

"Oh, okay," I say, and I let out a few fake laughs.

"Forget it," she says, disgusted. "You sound like a hyena."

She digs into her beach bag, finds the bottle of baby oil and iodine, and slathers herself with it—asks me to do her back. I look over at Greg. He's face down now on the blanket. His friend looks at me, smiles. I smile back.

"I'm hot . . . let's go swimming," I say.

"Not yet. I just got oiled up. Let's walk the beach."

"I thought we came to go swimming."

"We will. Just not right now. I don't want to look like a drowned rat."

While we're strolling along the shore, she tells me to look like I'm enjoying myself. "Just don't laugh," she says "and I'll kill you right here if you so much as glance in his direction."

"What's the *matter* with you?" I ask. "You're acting like he's royalty or something. I don't appreciate being treated like dirt. If you don't cut it out, I'll walk home and you can stay here all by yourself."

"Sorry," she says. "It's just that there are certain rules you have to follow to get a guy interested. I'm a little nervous, that's all."

"All right," I say, "just lighten up."

Every once in a while she stops, picks something up from the sand, and studies it as if she's really interested. When we're directly between Greg and the water, we stand forever examining a Pepsi cap. I glance up at his blanket and catch him staring straight at Eva. He looks at the sky and shades his eyes with his hand like he's watching an invisible jet plane pass overhead. It's then that I realize that Eva and Greg are playing the same game, and his friend and I have identical parts in it.

When we get back to our spot, Eva turns my radio on loud—*Rhythm of the Rain*. We lie on our stomachs. She works on her tan. I start reading *The Fountainhead*. It isn't long before we feel sand being kicked on our legs. A voice from above says, "Been sailing yet?"

Eva pretends she's sleeping, but I turn over and sit up—fast. I'm not crazy about people looking at my butt.

"Is your friend dead or just passed out?" he asks me.

I shake Eva's arm, and she acts as if she's annoyed because I woke her up. "What do you want? I just got to sleep."

I pick up my book, say nothing, pretend to read.

"My name's Greg Richards," he says. "I've seen you at the marina. Eva, right?"

"Yeah, that's right. What did you say your name was again?"

Give me a break, I think. *Where did she learn this crap?*

"Greg Richards—our parents know each other. Do you want to go for a swim?"

As I watch them walk toward the water, I think how things are changing and it makes me sad. When we're around boys,

I'm going to have to play second fiddle, but when it comes to Eva, I guess that's better than not being in the orchestra at all. I look over at Greg's friend. This time he doesn't smile and I don't smile back.

CHAPTER TWENTY-NINE

———◆———

I'M AT MY MOTHER'S wedding, standing next to her, holding her bouquet: sweetheart roses, pale peach. I'm not exactly what you would call relieved yet—the *I do* part is still to come. In the troublesome section of my head I can hear Mama saying *Nope, not going to do this, changed my mind.* Then she bolts out the back door of the church, her beige silk suit a blur. The heel of my dyed salmon pump is tapping the floor like a woodpecker. It's a good little while before I realize that I'm the one who's making the racket, and I tell myself to get a grip.

Finally, the preacher gets to the important part. My heart starts racing like when I used to go to the track with Manny and our long shot would take the lead. Then I hear "I now pronounce you man and wife." The words come through to my poor unbelieving mind, muffled and sluggish—somebody else's mother has just married the man of my dreams and I'm standing here pretending to be happy for her.

When Mr. Stephens kisses Mama he catches my eye, winks, and then I know it's safe to take the bulletproof vest off my heart. My brain wakes up from its coma, turns into a pompom girl, and keeps repeating the cheer it has practiced for so long: *Dad! Dad! Dad!*

* * *

Well, Mr. Pine doesn't know what he's talking about. The box
step will not get you anywhere as far as slow dancing is concerned. I think gym teachers should stick to teaching things you
do in a gym and not mess around with people's social lives. I'm
at the reception and I am really doing a job on Mr. Stephens'
new shoes.

"Oh, sorry," I say again after I have done *front together* when
I should have glided sideways.

"You're doing fine," he says. "Just relax, let yourself go loose.
That's the way."

Well, for goodness sake. When you stop telling your feet
where to go, they brush the chip off their shoulder and cooper-
ate. I think the school should have Mr. Stephens be the dance
teacher. If you get taught a thing in a kind, patient way, your
stubborn brain will say, *Okay, this I'll do.*

After the song is over, Mr. Stephens reclaims Mama. I walk
out onto the porch of the hotel, sit down in a huge wooden
rocking chair, and gaze across Lake Champlain to Vermont. It
is one of those postcard scenes where the sun is making stars
glitter on the water and the boats are bobbing along the waves
with their perky white sails—little dancing girls in starched
pinafores. Labor Day is just a few days away, and if you look
closely, you can spot some impatient trees that have already
started to get dressed up for the fall. My imagination lets me
smell burning leaves and taste the apple cider and cinnamon
doughnuts that go along with it. I think how lucky I am to have a
real father and to live in a place where the Adirondack autumns
are so beautiful they take your breath away. Sometimes God
just overwhelms me.

I walk back into the party, and for a minute, I think my eyes
are playing a joke on me. Grandma and Grandpa are dancing—close. He's holding her like she's the porcelain doll he mar-

ried, and this is *their* wedding all over again. She's staring up at him with a look on her face that I've never seen before—love, I think.

Hearts are funny things. They can be so broken and dead for such a long time, and then, when something comes along that's just right—a song maybe—they come alive and put themselves together like nothing bad ever happened.

*   *   *

Mama and Mr. Stephens are back from their weekend in Lake Placid and we're in my grandparents' living room picking up the last of our things when the phone rings. Mama answers and her face freezes into shock. She gives me such a look of fear that my heart stops and my brain tells me that Grandpa must be dead.

"Oh, hello, Mrs. Brand," she says, holding the phone so tightly that her knuckles are white. "Yes, it *has* been a long time. I did, on Saturday. John Stephens. He's a teacher at the campus school. Thank you, I'm sure I will be. Elizabeth? She's fine." Mama turns to me, gives me a beseeching look. "Yes, you're right. She is. I should have told you. I know how much it would have meant to you. I'm sorry. Of course. Just a minute."

She holds the phone by her waist, covers the mouthpiece. "Lizzy," she says, "it's for you. It's your grandmother Brand."

When she gives me the phone, I smile and let my hand touch hers softly. Before I say hello to Grammy Brand, I think now that Mama has trusted me with her secret, maybe someday I'll be able to tell her mine.